Situationz

Love, Lust, & Lies

J. Asmara

PUBLISHING

Lingering Secrets

Are you a product of upbringing or a product of self? Kayla Ferguson found herself on both sides of that question. Growing up all Kayla had was her mother Kathleen; who ran away from home at sixteen when she got pregnant with Kayla. Kathleen boarded a bus from Nashville, Tennessee and went to Atlanta, Georgia to be with a gentleman named Bryant that she met online. Kathleen realized that she made a mistake when Bryant's sweet helpful nature was quickly replaced by angry hurtful words and possessive behavior. Kathleen endured the mental and occasional physical abuse for three years before she freed herself from Bryant's grips. One night, Kathleen arrived home early from her waitressing job. She walked into the house and found Bryant in Kayla's room.

Kayla was naked on the bed and Bryant was fondling her.

"What in the fuck are you doing?" Kathleen exclaimed.

"Kat, it's not what it looks like," he tried to explain as he walked toward Kathleen.

"It looks like you were trying to fuck my baby," she said as she stormed to their bedroom and grabbed the gun from the night stand.

"Calm down," Bryant said as Kathleen cocked the gun.

"Don't tell me to calm down you sick motherfucker. Having the mom wasn't enough; you had to have the daughter too! You fucking pig! Get your ass on your knees."

"Kathleen."

"Shut the fuck up and get on your got damn knees before I fill your ass up with lead."

Lingering Secrets

Bryant complied with Kathleen's demand. With the gun pointed at his head, Kathleen called 9-1-1. "I caught this motherfucker playing with my two year old! Y'all better send someone to get him before I blow his brains out. The address is twenty thirty-seven Elm Street, apartment eight."

Kathleen hung up on the 9-1-1 operator and taunted Bryant. "You fucking predator. I should have known better from the start. You were a fucking twenty-five year old man, pursuing a sixteen year old girl. But I'd never thought that you would go after my baby. You sick fuck! You've made my life a living hell you bastard! Open your fucking mouth!"

"Kathleen baby, please calm down."

"Fuck you and your bull shit! Open your motherfucking mouth. I'm not going to say it a-fucking-gain."

Bryant opened his mouth and Kathleen

forced the barrel of the gun in his mouth.

"You cock-sucker! Suck it!" Bryant looked confused. "I said suck it. If you manage to keep your head by the time the police get here, you're going to need practice for all the dicks you'll be sucking in jail. When you're someone's bitch."

Kathleen battled with herself as she watched Bryant suck the gun. *Pull the trigger Kathleen. He will be one less pig in the world. Do it. Do it.* Kathleen was so focused that she didn't even hear when the police knocked on the door as she contemplated shooting him. Since she didn't answer, the officers kicked in the apartment door, ripping it off the chain. They made their way to the bedroom after they heard Bryant's muffled pleas. It wasn't until the third "Ma'am put the gun down and let us handle it" that Kathleen's mind snapped back to the situation. She was startled by the four police officers that were in her bedroom.

"Ma'am-" an officer stated.

"Okay. Okay," Kathleen said as she pulled the gun out of Bryant's mouth.

She was in the process of putting the gun on the ground when Bryant said, "That crazy bitch tried to kill me! Arrest her ass!"

Kathleen stopped and snapped, "Arrest me? You mother fucking pedophile! I'll blow your brains out! Fucking with my daughter! You're just like him!"

"Calm down ma'am. We're here to help. Put the gun down so we can get to the bottom of this."

"But-"

"Mommy!" Kayla yelled followed by her crying.

"Oh baby," Kathleen said walking to her naked daughter.

"Ma'am, I'm going to need that gun before you walk over to the child," a young officer said.

Kathleen looked at him with tears in her eyes. She handed the officer the gun and ran over to Kayla.

"Arrest that bitch!" Bryant exclaimed.

"Calm down sir," another officer said as he walked over to Bryant. "We got a call that you were acting inappropriately with a child and we need to get to the bottom of this."

"Acting inappropriately? He had his nasty ass fingers inside of her," Kathleen said as she covered Kayla with a blanket.

"Ma'am, can you and the child please come in the other room with me?" a female officer asked trying to separate Kathleen and Bryant so that she could get her statement.

Kathleen followed the officer to the kitchen. The officer asked basic questions such as: Kathleen's name, phone number, emergency information, and Kayla's full name and age. The officer took Kathleen's statement on the event.

"Ms. Alexander, I think I have all that I need as far as your statement and personal contact information. The next thing that we need to do is a sexual assault kit on Kayla."

"A sexual assault kit?"

"Yes. It will be done at the hospital. Qualified medical personnel will gather DNA and check her out to determine what all has been done to her. It is optional, but be aware Ms. Alexander that without it, the case against Mr. Nicholas will be your word against his. His word would probably include his fear for his life. As a mother, I understand, but know that we are blessing you this evening by not placing you in those silver bracelets due to the scene that we just witnessed. So, I hope you understand the importance of this kit."

"Yes."

"Great. Do you have transportation to the hospital or would you need me to take you?"

"I do not have a way. I need a ride please."

When they were done, Bryant was being escorted out of the apartment by the officers. "Stupid bitch! You aren't shit without me!"

"Sir. Calm down," an officer said.

"Slut bitch! Give my Kayla bear a kiss for me," he said with a sinister grin.

The officers rushed him out of the apartment. Kayla turned and held Kathleen tight around the neck.

"I'm sorry about that, Ms. Alexander. Go and get whatever you need for yourself and Kayla so that we can go to the hospital. Keep her wrapped in the blanket to maintain the integrity of any DNA that may still be on her."

"Okay," Kathleen said moving like a

zombie. *I've failed as a mother. I ain't shit just like my mother. She couldn't protect me and I did not protect my daughter.*

****

Kayla had faint memories of the incident. Over the course of her life, Kathleen had filled in the missing pieces. The sexual assault kit revealed that Kayla had extensive tearing in her vagina that resulted from Bryant using his fingers to penetrate her for the entire two years of her life. Kathleen then realized the abuse was the reason why Kayla had always developed what she thought was a diaper rash.

Bryant was indeed a predator. When the police searched their apartment they found nude photos of not only Kayla, but several other young children in a hidden compartment in the wood work of their bed. Bryant attempted to get an insanity plea but he was sentenced to twenty-five years on multiple counts of child pornography.

Kathleen wasn't the same after that night. She began to shut down and became incapable of providing the emotional support that Kayla desperately needed. Kayla was a strong girl though. She adapted to not having a mother and raised herself; all the while making excuses as to why Kathleen didn't express or hardly showed her any love.

The broken child grew into a broken young adult who longed for love. Unfortunately, Kayla didn't have a reference point for the love that she yearned for. Though, beautiful with her slender build, rich auburn hair, pouty lips, and green eyes, Kayla felt invisible most of her life. She was socially awkward and spent most of her alone time in her books. That in turn caused the other students to classify her as a geek. By Kayla's senior year of high school, she felt like she would be alone forever; but that changed when she met Ryan. One day, he walked into the convenience store where she worked.

"Hello beautiful," he said to a shocked Kayla. *There's no way that he's talking to me,* Kayla thought.

"Me?"

"Yes you. I don't see anyone else in here even close to as beautiful as you." Kayla's cheeks got rosy with his confirmation.

"Can I have your number so I can call you some time?"

"Okay," Kayla replied meekly.

He smiled and said, "I'm about to grab some beer so just have that ready for me."

Kayla wrote her number on a sheet of paper as Ryan walked around the store. He grabbed a six pack of Budweiser and a pack of Doritos chips. He placed the items on the counter and said, "I'm Ryan by the way."

"I'm Kayla."

"Nice to meet you."

"Nice to meet you too. I'll need to see your ID for the beer please."

"No problem babe. Here you go," he said as he pulled his license out of his pocket.

"Wow...Today is your birthday. Happy birthday," Kayla said as she looked at the ID.

"Thank you. I just made the big 2-1 and became the luckiest man on the planet."

"Cool. How'd you do that?" Kayla asked as she finished the transaction and also gave him the piece of paper with her number on it.

"I just met my future wife," he said with a wink. "What time do you get off?"

"Nine o'clock."

"I'll call you later," he said as he

walked out of the store.

Kayla let out a "yes" as she danced behind the counter. Her coworker came from out of the office and asked "Kayla, are you alright?"

"Yes, I'm actually better than alright," she said with a deep exhale.

****

Kayla and Ryan got hot and heavy throughout her senior year. Kathleen did not approve of their relationship at all. She could not get pass their age difference; she always flashed back to Bryant. "Mom, I'll be eighteen in a few months. It's only three years," Kayla would plead whenever Ryan's age would come up. It bothered Kayla because that was the only time Kathleen took a parental stance, but she understood why.

Kayla continued to see Ryan despite Kathleen's disapproval. She gave Ryan her virginity on prom night. She attempted to keep it from Kathleen, but she wasn't able too. When Kathleen found out she attempted to get Ryan arrested for statutory rape. But because Kayla was seventeen, she was considered a consenting adult so she attempted to put a restraining order on him. However, that did not go her way either, because no crime was committed. Kathleen was furious and had forbid Kayla to see him. However, Kayla continued to see Ryan behind her back. Unfortunately, Kayla had to let the cat out of the bag when she found out that she was pregnant a month before graduation. The conversation did not go well and it ended with Kathleen calling Kayla a "stupid bitch". It tore Kayla up inside. All she ever wanted was to feel loved by her mother. Kathleen did not utter a word to Kayla for two weeks.

Though her situation wasn't ideal, Kayla got through it with Ryan's support.

Kayla graduated and moved in with Ryan. He did not want Kayla to work while she was pregnant so she quit her job at the convenience store. Ryan worked as a mechanic at his family's shop.

During the pregnancy, Kayla and Kathleen slowly mended their broken relationship. By the time Kayla gave birth to her son Caleb, they were closer than they'd ever been. Kathleen took the role of a grandmother better than she handled her role as a mother.

Things in Kayla's life moved quickly. Six months after giving birth to Caleb, Kayla got pregnant with their daughter Christina. She and Ryan went to the court house and got married. Before she turned twenty-one she was a wife and mother of two.

Taking care of a family of four became stressful for Ryan. Every time Kayla suggested that she get a job to help out he'd go off on a tangent. His agitation quickly turned to verbal abuse. Kayla felt stuck. She had no one other than her mother; who always told her to stick it out. "Things will get better," Kathleen would always tell her.

Over the years, Ryan's beer to unwind at night turned into several beers and shots of liquor. It was fine with Kayla until his nights resulted in him going across her head. Kayla confided in Kathleen who told her that it was alright and to make it work with her husband because he was a "good" man. Kayla expected more than "stick it out" from her mother, but listened and hung in there for five additional years. She'd also endured at least a hundred beatings during that timeframe.

****

Kayla got back in the work force when Caleb and Christina were finally school age. She was working at a call center when the worst of the beatings occurred. She went to work with black and blue bruises on her face that she attempted to cover up with makeup. Her co-workers suspected that Kayla was getting abused but they'd rather whisper about it versus help her through it.

Kayla's supervisor, Ariel called her in her office when she saw Kayla one morning. "Have a seat Kayla." Kayla sat nervously.

"Did I do something wrong Ms. Brunson?"

"No. I called you in here to check on you. How are you Kayla?"

"I'm doing well."

"Are you sure?"

"Yes ma'am."

"Well I want to share something with you. About five years ago, I was in a toxic relationship. My ex was over protective, jealous, and physically abusive. I loved him dearly and because of that I made excuses for him. Everyone but me saw him for what he was worth. One night, I was working late and he thought that I was cheating on him with my co-worker. I went home to him in a jealous rage. I was tired from my long day so I did not argue with him. Unfortunately, he took that as me being guilty. He took out his gun and shot me in the head. Luckily, the bullet only grazed me. I fell to the ground and while I was down there, I witnessed him blow his brains out."

Kayla gasped and put her hands to cover her mouth. "That's awful Ms. Brunson," she said after a few second of awkward silence.

"Yes. It took me a while to get over it and honestly I'm still not completely over it because I still have nightmares. Kayla you are a smart and beautiful woman. Know that you are too great to be treated mediocre." Kayla shook her head. "I want you to take a sick day. Go somewhere and reflect on your life, your children, and your situation. Here is my personal cell phone number. Call me anytime."

"Thank you Ms. Brunson," Kayla said fighting back her tears.

"You're welcome Kayla and I mean anytime. Alright?"

"Okay."

Kayla left out of Ariel's office and quickly walked to her car, where she sat and cried. Ariel's story was a reality check. "What are you doing Kayla? You have kids to think about."

She wiped the tears off her face and drove to Kathleen's house to tell her that she was going to leave Ryan and needed to move in for a while. When Kayla pulled up to Kathleen's house, Ryan's pickup truck was in the driveway. *Why isn't he at work? Guess mom needed him to do something.*

Guess I'll be letting him know that I'm leaving him too, Kayla thought. She took a deep breath before she got out of the car.

She used her key and went into the house. She looked in the living room and then the kitchen, but there was no sign of Kathleen or Ryan. She heard muffled voices coming from the den. She made her way down the hall to the den. She entered the room and saw Kathleen bent over the sofa and Ryan was fucking her from behind. Kayla was horrified.

"So this is why you didn't want me to leave him!" she exclaimed. Kathleen and Ryan were both startled by her outburst.

"Kayla-" "Baby-" they both started as Kayla said, "Fuck you both! Y'all deserve each other!"

Kayla stormed out of the house and slammed the door behind her. She hopped in her car and sped away leaving Kathleen speechless and Ryan attempting to get dressed. Kayla was five miles up the road by the time Ryan got out of Kathleen's house. She stopped in a Wal-Mart parking lot and attempted to get her thoughts together.

"I can't fucking believe this!" she screamed as she started to cry.

Thoughts bounced all around her head while she sat there with visions of her mother and husband. When Kayla finally looked at her watch she realized that she'd been there for an hour. She felt defeated and did not know what to do or where to go. Kathleen was all she had. Kayla looked at the piece of paper in her center console with Arial's number on it. She picked it up and grabbed her cell phone. She'd had a total of twenty-nine missed calls between Ryan and Kathleen.

"Motherfuckers," she said as she dialed Arial's number.

"Arial speaking, can I help you?"

"Ms. Brunson this is Kayla."

"Okay. Give me a second and let me get back to my office."

Kayla heard sounds as Arial moved back to her office from the copy machine. "Okay, I'm back. Are you okay Kayla?"

"No," she responded sadly.

"What happened?"

"I left and thought about what you shared with me. I decided I was going to leave Ryan's sorry ass. I went to my mother's to tell her that I needed to stay with her for a while. When I got there, I found my husband fucking my mother from behind."

"Oh my god. You poor girl!"

"I'm done with the both of them. But I don't know what to do. I don't have anyone else," she said crying again.

"I'm sorry Kayla. That's awful but you have to pull yourself together. What time do the kids get out of school?"

"Three o'clock."

"Are you sure you want to leave your husband?"

"I am a thousand percent sure."

"Okay. I have a place where you and your children can go. It's called Melrose Manor. It's a home that is designed to help women who have suffered with addiction and abuse."

"I don't know. Is a place like that safe for my children?"

"Yes it is. Trust me. Pick your children up from school and meet me at twenty-four eighty-seven Elwood Street, in Marietta. Don't worry about packing anything. I will make sure that you and the kids have what y'all need."

"Okay."

"Call me if you have any hiccups. See you soon," Arial said as she hung up.

A slight calm came over Kayla. She picked up Caleb and Christina from school. Once she did, they bombarded her with questions about why she picked them up early and asked where they were going. Kayla tried not to take her emotions out on them but they worked her last nerve, "Shut y'all mouths and let me drive." Kayla rarely snapped at them so they were in shock that she had yelled at them. They immediately sat back, shut their mouths, and stared out of the window.

Kayla pulled up to a nice sized two story house with a wraparound porch.

"Whoa," Christina said.

"Whoa is right," Kayla whispered to herself.

Arial came out of the house and walked to the car with a big smile on her face. "I'm glad you made it. Come on out. Don't be afraid."

Kayla unbuckled her seat belt and said, "Okay. Kids let's go," to Christina and Caleb.

They all got out of the car as Arial continued, "Oh my, they are so cute Kayla."

"This is Christina and this is Caleb," Kayla said showcasing her kids.

"Hi, I'm Ms. Arial. I'm a friend of your mom and this is my place," she said pointing to the house.

Her place? Kayla thought.

"This is Melrose Manor. Do y'all want to look around?"

"Yes!" Christina and Caleb yelled.

Ariel walked them to the porch that had a swing and several rocking chairs. They entered through the front door into a big open room that was separated into two sitting areas. One had a big sectional and a large flat screen television and the other had a sofa, bean bag chairs, a television, and game section. "This is our lounge and play areas." She walked us over to a small office area and said, "We have movies, books, and games stored in here along with the computer. The key has to be signed out; there will always be at least one attendant here."

Arial moved along to the kitchen. There was a woman coming out of the pantry. "This is Candice, my head attendant. Candice this is Kayla, Christina, and Caleb."

"Hi everyone," Candice said with a smile. "Welcome to Melrose Manor."

"Thank you," Kayla said.

Arial continued their tour with the laundry area, seven bedrooms, five bathrooms, the basement, and back yard. Arial and Kayla let the kids play on the swing set as they talked.

"So what do you think Kayla?"

"It's beautiful but I don't know. I've never stayed in a place like this? What about the kids? And their school?"

"Well, this place is safe from your

abusive husband. There are four ladies and five children here already so there's room for you and the kids. Not to mention, they have been kept safe also. I know it's scary but a place like this is what saved me from going down the wrong road after my "Nick" situation. I was a mess. I started using drugs and lost everything. I cannot make you stay, but just know that you are welcome. We offer six month stays. It gives the ladies enough time to get on their feet. We also make exceptions on a case by case basis."

Kayla looked at her children as they played. She never stood up for herself her whole life and she decided that day was the day. "Alright. I will stay."

"Cool. Let me show you to your room. You can leave the kids back here if you'd like."

They walked inside the house and she told Candice, "I'm showing Kayla to her room. Keep an eye on the children in the backyard."

"Yes ma'am."

Arial took Kayla to a room that had an on-suite bathroom. "This will be your room. I try to give the women with children private bathrooms." There were two twin size beds in the room. "We have cots if this is not enough sleeping space for you. Quick rules, curfew is at nine pm unless you have a night job. But you don't have that problem since you work for me. Also, fighting is not allowed. If you have a problem with one of the ladies, let one of the attendants know. Make sure that you clean up behind yourself; the attendants are here to make sure that everything runs smoothly, not to be a maid to anyone. Lastly, treat this place like it's your home because it is."

"Thank you so much, Ms. Brunson. I'm so grateful for your kindness."

"No problem. Here are three Wal-Mart gift cards for you and the children; there is one for a hundred dollars and two for fifty dollars. Go get some clothes and under garments for you and the children. There are toothbrushes, toothpaste, deodorant, tampons, and pads in the closet inside of the bathroom, so don't worry about those things. Wal-Mart is right up the street."

"I don't know how I can ever repay you."

"Just be the person you are destined to be and that will be payment enough for me. I have to get back to the office. I want you to take tomorrow off and register the children here for school. I'll have Candice help you with that also."

"Okay."

"See you later."

Kayla, Christina, and Caleb settled into Melrose Manor and within a month, things had started to look promising for Kayla.

Arial referred her to a social worker who arranged a mutual location for Kayla and Ryan's visitation with the children, as well as child support payments. Work was also going well; Arial never spoke of Melrose Manor nor treated her any differently. Kayla even made friends with the women; especially a woman named Serena who had a similar situation.

****

Kayla's smooth sailing came to a halt during her third month at Melrose. She received an alarming phone call from her mother's neighbor while she was at work.

"Hello, Mrs. Emery." Kayla paused and her mouth fell open, "What? I'll be right there."

Kayla went to Arial's office and from there she rushed to her mother's home. There was an ambulance, two police cars, and a fire truck parked along the road. Kayla got out of the car and ran to the front door when a firefighter grabbed her arm. "Ma'am you cannot go in there."

"The hell I can't, this is my mother's house."

"Calm down ma'am, let me get someone that can speak to you." He let her arm go and went inside to get a police officer, but Kayla was right on his heel. There were emergency workers all throughout the house. The fireman realized that Kayla was behind him but decided not to try and stop her at that point. He introduced her to the first respondent officer.

"Hello, Ms..."he said extending his hand.

"Kayla. What happened?"

"It appears that your mother died in her sleep. Her neighbor called us when she hadn't seen her."

"Oh no."

"We believe that she passed away two,

maybe three days ago." Kayla began to cry. Though she hated what Kathleen did, she was still her mother.

"Come have a seat."

"No. I want to see her."

"Are you sure?"

"Yes." He escorted her to Kathleen's bedroom.

She walked in and saw Kathleen laying there with a pale look and a gray tint to her skin. Kayla walked over to her and touched her cool skin. "No," she whispered in a flat monotone voice as tears fell. She stood there and cried for a few minutes before the officer told her that they needed to process the body.

Kayla went into the living room as they worked to remove Kathleen's body. She sat there with a blank stare during the process.

"Ma'am. We're done and have cleared out all of our equipment. Do you need anything? Maybe you want me to contact someone for you?" Kayla snapped out of her trance, though she still had a blank expression. She did not respond, the officer said, "Ma'am."

"Huh?"

"We are leaving. Do you need anything? Do you need me to call anyone for you?"

Her voice cracked slightly as she said, "No. I'll be alright."

"Alright, ma'am. Here's my card and if you need anything don't hesitate to call me."

"Thank you."

"I'm sorry again for your loss." Kayla forced a smile as he walked out of the house.

She sat in the house for a while until she gained enough mental strength to leave. She ensured that the house was locked up completely, and then drove to Melrose Manor.

Her phone rang as she was on the highway. "Hello," she answered.

"Is everything alright, Kayla? How's your mom?" Arial asked.

"Not too good. She's dead."

"Oh my. I'm so sorry," Arial said sincerely. "Well, that makes what I'm about to say a little awkward."

"What?"

"The mail was just delivered and there's a letter addressed to you. It's from your mother."

"What?"

"Yes."

"I'm on my way to Melrose Manor, but I can turn back around."

"No. You should go and prepare yourself to deal with the children. I'll bring it."

"Are you sure? I don't-"

"Yes I'm sure."

"Thank you. Thank you for everything

you've done for me. I'm forever in debt to you."

"No, you're not. You just make sure that you take care of yourself and those children. Okay?"

"Okay," Kayla said with a smile.

****

Kayla was on the porch in a rocking chair when Arial pulled up to the house. She handed Kayla the letter and said, "I have to get back to the office so I can't stay. Call me if you need me." Arial gave her a hug and left. Kayla took a deep breath, opened the envelope, pulled out the letter, and read it.

Kayla,

Writing this letter is very hard for me to do, but I know that it has to be done. I'm not going to say sorry for the things I've done in the past because I honestly think that I'm incapable of feeling any remorse, or any other emotion for that matter. It's sad but true. There are things that you do not know about me and my past. So here it is. As a young girl I was daddy's little girl; his little "princess". Those were the good days. Mama used to call me spoil, but I didn't care because I knew that my daddy loved me. I just didn't know how much. Daddy would bathe me and tuck me in every night. He made sure that he was the one to lotion me; while exploring my developing body. My mom was an airhead wino so she never noticed. When I turned fourteen we had "the talk". Daddy's version included a show and tell of the things boys would want to do. "You make sure that you don't give yourself to any of those boys because you are daddy's special girl," he'd said. I agreed and he kissed me like no dad should ever kiss his daughter. Let's just say that I lost my virginity that night to my father. I knew deep down that it was wrong but he was my dad and I was loyal to him. He took me as often as he wanted too. When I got pregnant with you, he threw a big stink about me whoring around with boys at school. But that show was for my mama because he knew he left no room for me to be with anyone else. Though his words and actions hurt me, they were what I needed to break free from the hold that he had on me. I ran away; unfortunately to that snake Bryant. He was a different kind of predator. I know this may be a lot Kayla, but I hope you can understand why I've hid it from you all of these years. I never felt there was a right time to say "Well, the reason I never bring up your father is because he is also your grandfather." I failed as a mother because I never knew what a mother was. My mother was a drunk who didn't care about anything outside of her wine. By the time you get this, I will be gone. I could not do right by you in life so here is my attempt in death. I *put your name on the house about a year ago so it is now yours. I also left you an insurance policy worth two hundred and fifty thousand dollars. Use that to take care of my beautiful grandchildren. I told you to stay with Ryan for my own selfish reason. That was wrong of me. You deserve better. Divorce his sorry ass. I am feeling sadness so I guess that I'm not completely lost. So here I go at my attempt of remorse. I'm sorry, baby. Burn this when you are done because the police will not suspect a suicide and this letter will bring a reason for an autopsy. Take care of yourself.*

Mom

Kayla attempted to process all that Kathleen had said in her goodbye letter as she sat in the rocking chair. She always thought that she was the product of a high school crush or even a one night stand gone wrong. The thought of her being the product of rape never crossed her mind.

She sat and cried until Candace came out and asked if she was okay. Kayla wiped her snot and tears with the sleeve of her shirt and said "yes". She got up, went inside of the house to the fireplace, placed the letter in, and set it ablaze. Kayla stood in silence as the truth of her and her mother's past burned.

Dangerously In Love

Hope sat in the garden taking in the rays of the sunshine. She smiled at a young boy who picked a few flowers out of the garden.

"Tommy, no. You can't pick the people's flowers," his mother said as she waved him away from the garden.

"But I wanted to get them for your Mommy," Tommy replied.

"Oh honey. You're so sweet."

Hope reflected on her life. She thought about her daughter Chastity, because she used to do gestures like him when she was younger. Unfortunately, at that time Hope and Chastity's relationship was nowhere as sweet as that. Like Hope's mama always told her, "Things are always good until they're not."

****

Hope was a teenage mother. She had

Chastity just before her seventeenth birthday; twelve days to be exact. Being a teenage mother was not ideal for her but she made the decision to not abort the baby. Her mother Alice, nor Chastity's father, Terrance was happy about the decision. Alice, who was also a teenage mother, didn't want Hope to experience the challenges that she once experienced. However, Terrance's reason was more of a selfish one.

The twenty-nine year old hustler was married with two children. That tidbit of information was not shared with Hope until she delivered Chastity. Terrance's lies caught up with him, and his wife Erica got a whiff of the affair. She followed him to the hospital. Once she got there, she announced to him and Hope that she was putting him out. Hope was crushed by the information. Terrance preyed on her naïve nature and convinced her that he was sorry and wanted their family. Then he played house with her long enough to plead his way back home with Erica; leaving Hope and Chastity high and dry.

Hope used the hurt that he brought her to fuel her willingness to succeed. With her mother's help, she graduated high school and continued her education in the nursing field. Her hard work and determination paid off and she became the head neonatal nurse at St. Joseph's Hospital when Chastity was ten years old.

Hope believed that Chastity saved her life and she owed her the best life possible. She dedicated all of her time to work and Chastity. She kept her circle small by not having many friends or a dating life. Though Chastity appreciated her mother, she felt guilty that she did not have a life. "I'll 'live' once you're grown," she'd say whenever Chastity would bring up her going out. She would pick up on

Hope's tone and let up and drop the situation.

Once Chastity turned eighteen and almost "grown" she pushed harder to get Hope "wifed" up as she called it. She enlisted her godmother and Hope's childhood friend, Monica to help her. When Monica brought the idea to Hope she shut it down quickly.

"I'm good Monica. I don't need a man."

"Shitting me that you don't! When was the last time you had someone knock the dust off that thing?"

"It's not about that Monica. I have to make sure Chastity is good. Plus I have a vibrator or two," Hope added with a giggle.

"First off, Chastity IS good. You raised her right Hope. She'll be graduating in a few months. Second off, I know you're tired of buying batteries!"

"Whatever! Shut up!"

"But for real, just think about it. You

better start using all that sexiness you got going on before you lose it. Your ass could end up busted up like me," Monica said showcasing her body.

"Whatever, chick. You are not busted up. You're bigger than you were but you're still bad. You know that though. You're just always fishing for compliments."

Monica laughed and said, "True."

"I don't have time to play with you. I have to get ready for work."

"Okay."

The situation wasn't quite like how Chastity or Monica thought. Hope carried the secret of her and Terrance's rendezvous throughout the years. After he left, Terrance later returned to Hope's life when Chastity was twelve years old.

Hope saw Terrance at the hospital when his mother had a stroke. She was in the cafeteria on her break when he walked in. She damn near choked when he walked up to her. She had mixed emotions when she looked up at him but lucky for him she didn't curse him out. One, because the sane part of her told her he wasn't worth it and the second reason was because she was at her place of employment. He sat with her and they talked like old friends catching up. Besides the update on his mother's health, he also shared that he and Erica were still married. Not happily according to him, but none the less still together.

They exchanged numbers that day and had occasional conversations. His mother died six months after their reconnection. Terrance called Hope and used her for comfort. They met up that night and the visit ended with them unleashing their bottled up sexual tension for one another that they'd carried with them for those many years.

Their relationship continued and

consisted of him providing support for Chastity behind Erica's back and him also providing his services to Hope sexually when she needed a tune up. Though it was wrong and unconventional, Hope liked their situation. Everyone in her life hated Terrance for what he did to her and Chastity and that was why she held on to her secret.

Hope and Monica chatted some more and ended the call on an "agree to disagree" note. Hope dismissed the conversation like she did the many others they'd had, about her lack of a love life.

All of that changed within a month, at a birthday gathering that Monica had at her house. Hope was sitting at a table in the corner when a tall dark and extremely handsome man walked in. "Damn he's fine," she heard one of Monica's associates say to one of her girlfriends. "Yes he is," her friend cosigned. "Isn't he the doctor?"

another asked. Hope sat quietly not entertaining the ladies, but could not help but admire how attractive the stranger was.

Hope walked and mingled at the party trying not to be a party pooper but she was ready to make a B-line home to put on her pajamas and watch her DVR recordings. Every time she mentioned anything about being tired or wanting to leave, Monica would ask her to stay.

Monica and Hope were in the kitchen when Mr. Tall Dark and Handsome walked in.

"Hey Myron," Monica said. "Can I get you something?"

"Nah baby girl, I'm good. Just wanted a few minutes to officially wish you a happy birthday," he said handing her a card.

"Thank you," she replied with a hug. "I want you to meet someone. This is my best friend, Hope. Hope this is Myron

Jacobs."

"Nice to meet you," Hope said.

"Nice to meet you too," he replied with a kiss to her hand.

The gesture sent a fire through her body but Hope kept her composure.

"What a nice way to greet someone."

"Yes it is, when the person is beautiful as you."

"Ah shit," Monica mumbled.

"You're quite a charmer, Mr. Jacobs."

Myron gave her a million dollar smile and then said, "I'll let you two get back to your conversation. I'm about to get out of here. I'll catch you later, Monica."

"Okay Myron. Thanks for coming."

"Thanks for the invite," he said as he headed toward the doorway to the kitchen. Midway he stopped and turned, "I hope that I'm not being to forward but you're very intriguing and I'd love to get to know you better if that's okay?"

"Well..." Hope said stunned by his words. "I'm really not interested in getting to know anyone." Monica nudged her with her elbow. "What? I'm not."

"You should be though," Monica mumbled.

Myron stood and watched their brief exchange. "Well, how about I leave you my card?"

"Okay."

He went into his pocket and pulled out a business card. "Just know that I will be looking forward to hearing from you," he mentioned when he handed the card to Hope.

"I will keep that in mind."

"Until then," he said as he left out of the kitchen.

"Girl you be tripping," Monica said. "A fine ass man tries to get at you and you acting stank."

"Whatever. Nobody was acting stank,"

Hope replied with an eye roll. "He was fine though. What's his deal?"

"He's a chiropractor and single with no kids."

"A chiropractor? Nice. How old is he? He looked a little young. You know I don't do young men."

"He's younger than us, but he's not *young*."

"What's not young?"

"He's twenty-seven."

"Twenty-seven!?! He's a baby Monica!"

"Stop it. Did you think of him being a baby when he was up in here just now? My eyes work just like yours and he is FULLY grown. Stop tripping. You need to get your groove back anyway, Stella. Get some dust knocked off that thing!" Monica said with a laugh. "He's mature, has a career, and is sexy as hell so I don't see the problem. Plus, he said he'd like to get to know you not sweep you off your feet and marry you. You're always over thinking things. Stop it. Do some crazy shit every once in a while."

Monica poured herself a drink, "Get some young dick and be happy for once."

Hope laughed at Monica but knew that she was dead serious. She had one last drink with Monica before heading home.

****

Hope finally decided to give Myron a call. The conversation was engaging and she accepted a date request. Since then, they'd gone out several times over the course of a month. She'd kept the relationship hushed from Chastity, because she didn't want her to read too much into what she and Myron were doing. However, Chastity wasn't focused on that anyways because she was stressed out by her own extracurricular activities.

Hope was strict when it came to Chastity and her dating. Her philosophy was that school came first. Chastity had her whole life to worry about men and relationships. Chastity always agreed with Hope when she spoke to her about boys, so Hope never thought that she would go against her wishes.

The truth of the matter was that while Hope thought that Chastity was in bed dealing with menstrual cramps, she was actually feeling the after effects of an abortion. She had been sneaking around with a guy named MJ that she met at the bookstore in the mall. He entertained her while her mother was at work. It was all fun and games, until her period was late. Her stomach sunk in when she got a positive result from the pregnancy test.

MJ was excited when she told him. She quickly dismissed his joy and brought up the fact that she was months away from graduation and then planned to go to college. Those things were true, but her main reason was because she was not as emotionally attached as MJ was. She saw a good time and money while he saw a future together. Against everything in him, he gave Chastity the four hundred dollars for the abortion. A decision that she knew would haunt her forever.

Hope knocked on Chastity's bedroom door as she laid there reflecting back on the decision that she made.

"Come in," Chastity said as cheery as she could."

"Are you okay sweetie? Do you want me to get you some hot tea or something?"

"No. I'll be alright. I took some pills and I'm just waiting on them to kick in."

"Are you sure?"

"Yes. You look nice. Are you going out with your mystery man?"

"What mystery man? I don't know what you're talking about."

"I'm not blind Ma. You're on the phone

late nights, coming in from work in different clothes than you left in, and you be having a real cheesy grin on your face."

"So you think you have all the answers huh, smarty pants?"

"You're a little too jazzy to be sitting around the house. Sooooooo…"

"So, nothing. There's nothing to tell. While you're all in my business, you need to worry about feeling better."

"Okay Ma," Chastity said leaving the situation alone. Seeing as she had her secrets, she respected Hope for keeping hers also.

****

"Baby do you have to go? I'm getting tired of you running out on me like you're Cinderella. You sure you don't have a husband? Twelve kids?" he asked playfully.

"No. Cut it out Myron. I told you, I'm very cautious about who I bring around my daughter. You know I have to leave because my daughter graduates tomorrow. Please continue being patient with me," she said with a kiss.

"You don't have to worry about that. I'm not going anywhere."

Hope smiled at his statement and kissed Myron again. She was happy that she gave him a chance, because he was good to her. They'd gotten really close and the relationship was moving rather quickly. Nothing was too big or small when it came to Hope. Myron had gotten to the point in his life where he really wanted a relationship. Hope embraced and appreciated his honesty. He shared with her that his last relationship ended with him being used and abused. Because of that, she ended her sneaking around with Terrance; not before one last session of him in the bedroom of their frequented hotel.

Terrance did not take the news very well. Though he played the macho role, he continued calling with his low-key begging sessions. Though the dick was superb, Hope fought her urges and stayed true to what she and Myron were building together.

As Myron walked her to the door, he spun her around and said, "I have something to ask you."

"What is it honey?"

Hope was shocked when she saw Myron get on one knee. "What are you doing? I-"

"Shhhhh...I'm doing what my heart has told me to do," Myron said as he pulled out and opened a ring box. "Baby I love you. My life has been wonderful since you entered it. Please be my wife."

"I...I...but it's so soon."

"There's no time frame on what I feel and I know you feel it too. Baby, please."

Hope was torn. Her heart was telling her go for it and her mind was telling her, Hell no! *What's a girl to do?* As she opened her mouth to respond she replayed Monica's word, "stop over thinking everything". Before she knew it the word "yes" popped out.

"Yes?" Myron eagerly asked.

Holy shit. "Yes," she said reassuring Myron as well as herself.

Myron put the one carat princess cut diamond ring on her finger and then embraced her in a kiss. "Baby you won't regret it. I will make you the happiest woman on the planet."

Little did Myron know, Hope had already regretted the decision that she made. She had not even told Chastity about Myron, let alone talked to her about thinking about getting engaged. She had no idea on how the conversation was going to start or end.

Situationz

Hope and Monica sat in the auditorium waiting for the graduation ceremony to start. "I'm still shocked right now Hope," Monica said in reference to the spontaneous engagement.

"Me too, shit."

"When are you going to tell Chas and Mama Gloria?"

Hope was still up in the air about it. When she got home the night before, Chastity was already in bed asleep. Then she left early that morning in preparation for her afternoon graduation. Hope decided to take the ring off and leave it in her jewelry box until she told everyone. Though she didn't know the how, she definitely knew the when; that day. Hope was now worried because Myron insisted on meeting her mother and daughter. *Lord help me,* she thought to herself.

"It will have to be today Monica,

because Myron is not letting this slide without me telling the ones that I love about him. Damn."

"Why are you acting like a teenager who needs to tell her mom? Sweetie you're grown. Not only are you grown, you're the shit! You've done well for yourself so stop tripping. Are you happy?"

"Yes."

"Then excuse my French, fuck everyone who goes against that. Straight fuck them with a stiff dick."

Hope had to laugh at her, but she was right. She was dang near forty years old, with a career, and handled all of her responsibilities on her own. Her smile quickly disappeared once she felt a tap on her shoulder.

When she turned around it was none other than Terrance. "What are you doing here?" she asked between clinched teeth.

"What do you mean 'what am I doing

here?' I do have a daughter graduating today, right?"

"You don't have shit here," Monica interjected with.

"Chill Monica," Hope said to her. "Really Terrance? This is the time that you decide to make an appearance? Is this really what we're doing?"

"Yes. So are you going to let me in the row or do I need to sit behind you?"

"You need to take your ass somewhere else," Monica mumbled under her breath.

Hope moved down so that he could sit in the row with her. She watched Monica as she rolled her eyes. *I'm really not up for this shit today,* Hope thought. They all sat in silence until Hope's mother came. *Oh boy,* Hope thought as she looked at her mother's face.

"Hello Ms. Alice," Terrance said as he stood up to greet her.

Alice ignored his kind gesture and

turned to Hope, "What is this lying, no good, piece of crap, doing here at my granddaughter's graduation?"

"He is her father Mother."

"No he is not. He is her sperm donor who has not laid eyes on his child since she was a year old. Or have you forgot, that he abandoned you and my grand baby?"

"Look Ms. Alice-"

"No, I got this," Hope said to Terrance with a finger shake. "Look Mother, today is not the day for this. It is Chastity's day, so we are all going to act civilized as we watch my baby walk across that stage."

Alice pierced her lips together and sat in her seat "Humph."

Hope didn't want to put her mother in her place like that because she was only trying to protect her and Chastity, but the graduation ceremony was not the time nor the place to get into it. But it bothered the hell out of Hope because she knew that Terrance really didn't give a damn about Chastity. Over the years of them messing around, he never once mentioned meeting her. He was content with being in the background for so many years, but all of a sudden he wanted to be involved since Hope had cut him off.

Hope focused on the stage. She was filled with excitement during the graduation that she'd almost forgot that Terrance was there with his bullshit. Hope, Alice, and Monica crowded Chastity when she made her way over to them.

"I'm so proud of you baby girl," Hope said glowing with pride.

"Thanks Ma," she said giving Hope a big hug.

"You did it," Alice said. "Come give grandma some love, my baby."

"Then bring it around to give godma some love, my little jelly bean."

Chastity made her rounds with hugs and kisses to everyone except Terrance. They were all engaged in pictures and conversation when Terrance let out an attention grabbing cough reminding them that he was there. *Here we go,* Hope thought as she looked at him.

"Baby girl, I have someone that I would like for you to meet. This is your father, Terrance Walker."

"Father?" she asked with a look of confusion.

"Yes," Terrance interjected. "Nice to meet you," he said with his arms open for a hug.

Chastity stood guarded. "Wish I could say the same," she replied.

"Chastity!" Hope yelled.

"What Ma? I don't know this dude. He's been missing in action my whole childhood and now that I've graduated high school he pops up? He missed out on the phase of my life when I wanted and needed a father. Now I am a grown woman who knows better. So, if you welcome him back with open arms then that's fine. But I'm not. So where are we eating at because I'm starving?"

"Red Lobster," Alice said as she grabbed Chastity's hand and walked toward the exit with Monica walking right behind them.

"Well..." Terrance said to Hope once they were alone.

"Well what? Did you think that you could walk your ass up in here and play 'Super Dad'? Why did you even come? I thought you were content with not being in her life? "

"I was."

"Until?"

"Until now. Shit. Don't be questioning me," he snapped.

"Until now huh?" Hope said with a

head nod. "Hmmm...until I decided to stop fucking with you right?"

"Whatever, Hope. Don't flatter yourself."

"If you say so. So, what now?"

"What do you mean?"

"Chastity didn't fall for your charming good looks so what now? Are you going back in the dark?"

"No, I'm not. I want to be in her life." Terrance fumbled around with a button on his shirt before he said, "Honestly Hope, the past few months I've been doing a lot of thinking. At first it had a lot to do with you deciding to stop fucking with me, but then I started reflecting back on the fucked up things I've done in my life. You're a good woman and I should not have left you to handle our responsibility alone. She's beautiful, smart, not on drugs, and not a teenage mother so I salute you for doing such a great job."

"Well thank you," Hope said. She was left in shock of the softer side of Terrance. Was it possible for him to get it together? She hoped so, but still didn't completely believe everything that he was saying.

"Thank you. I want to thank you for being you, Hope. I know I've messed up, but I'm going to do whatever I have too, to make it right."

Hope decided to try him and his sincerity, "Okay that sounds great. Since you're here, I have to tell you something."

"What?"

"I'm getting married."

"What!?! To who? I figured that a man was the reason why you left me."

"Left you? Terrance have you forgotten that you have a wife and two kids my dear?" Terrance rolled his eyes and began to pout. Hope's cell phone rang. It was Alice. "Hello...I'm on my way out now," she said quickly before hanging up. "I have to leave now. I truly hope that you are serious and we are able to work something out with our daughter."

Terrance forced a smile and quickly nodded his head. "See you later, Hope," he said softly.

"See you later, Terrance."

Hope walked off leaving Terrance to deal with his emotions. As far as he knew (in his mind anyway), Hope was forever his.

****

It was finally time for Myron to meet the family. After talking about Terrance's reappearance, during their after graduation lunch, Hope told her family about her engagement to him. Though they were shocked and somewhat worried about the secrecy, they trusted her judgment and were excited to see who had broke through her harden exterior.

They pulled up in front of Alice's

house. "Are you ready baby?" Hope asked.

"Of course darling."

"I hope so," Hope whispered before she landed a kiss to Myron's lips.

"Hmmmm…Are you ready my future?"

"As ready as I can be," Hope said with a smile.

"Let's go then," he replied as he got out of the car and walked over to the passenger side to open Hope's door.

The two of them walked up to the front door hand in hand. Hope took a deep breath before she pressed the doorbell. "Hey," Alice said with a huge smile on her face when she opened the door. "Come in."

"Mom this is Myron. Myron this is my mother Alice Scott."

"Nice to meet you Ma'am."

"Nice to meet you too. From what Hope told me you will be my son-in-law pretty soon, so no need for the formalities. Call me Alice."

Myron flashed Alice a huge smile. "He's cute," Alice mouthed to Hope as she escorted them to her living room. "Everyone, they are here," she announced. "This is Myron. Myron this is everyone; my best friend Sophie, her daughter Amber and her friend Ben, you know Monica, and my granddaughter should be coming downstairs in a minute."

Everyone said hello and gave them both hugs and handshakes. Everyone was in a gaggle around Myron when Chastity walked in. Hope caught a glimpse of her and moved toward her. "Hey, baby girl. I want you to come over here and meet Myron."

Hope and Chastity walked over to the spot where Ben and Myron were engaged in a conversation. "Baby," Hope said once she approached him. "This is my baby girl, Chastity. Chastity this is Myron."

"Nice to..." Myron started to say while

he was turning completely around. Once his and Chastity's eyes met, he was not able to finish his sentence.

After a brief awkward silence Chastity said, "Nice to meet you too."

"Same here he said slowly."

"Excuse me, but I have to run," Chastity said.

"Run where?" Hope asked.

"Ma…"

"Don't ma me. You're grown but I still worry."

"I know Ma. I'm about to go by Vivian's."

"Let me talk to you," Hope said. She and Chastity moved into the kitchen. "Do you really have to go to Vivian's? I really want you to stay and get to know Myron Chastity. He's going to be a part of your life as well as mine."

"Yes. You guys enjoy your evening and I will see you at home later," Chastity said with an attitude.

"Okay whatever," Hope said and walked off. She decided to not let Chastity and her teenage attitude take her joy away. She went back to the living room to Myron.

"Is everything alright?" he asked.

"Yes."

"Your daughter doesn't seem to like me. Did she say anything?

"No, but no worries. For the most part, Chastity is a good kid except her occasional attitude. She's a teenager and that's what they do. Are you sure this is what you want to walk into?"

"The only thing I'm sure of right now is that I am in love with you. Anything outside of that will work itself out."

A confident grin covered Hope's face. She had no concerns at that moment.

****

Hope told Myron instead of having a large wedding that she'd rather use the money for a honeymoon and to purchase a new home. So they had a simple wedding at a local wedding chapel and then went to Spain for a week. She hoped that by the time they returned from the trip that Chastity would come around to the idea of her being married now. Unfortunately, that did not happen and instead their relationship took a turn for the worst. Their conversations were few in numbers and brief. Chastity spent most of her time at school, working, or at her friend Vivian's apartment.

"Baby, I just don't know what's up with her." Hope said to Myron speaking about her and Chastity's relationship. "It's like she turned eighteen and turned into a different person."

"I wouldn't worry about it too much sweetness. I'm sure things will get better in time," he said with a soft kiss to her neck. "Trust me." Myron knew he had a lot to do with the problem so he'd made up in his mind that he'd speak to her.

The next day, Myron did just that. The much needed conversation took some of the tension away from the situation, and things were a little better. Hope no longer felt like she was being tugged in the middle by her husband and daughter. Life was good.

****

Over the next four years, things went well between the three of them. Chastity was doing well in college, Myron had doubled his patient list, and Hope accepted a promotion at work. It was also a promotion that kept her away from home. Hope and Myron held it down in their new home together while Chastity did the same in a townhouse near the campus.

Hope never really understood Alice's saying, "Things are always good until they ain't," until one day when Myron came home and told her, "We need to talk."

"What's going on?" Hope asked as she took a seat on the couch. She quickly became anxious as she watched Myron pace back and forth in front of her. "What Honey?"

"I have something to tell you. It's hard because I don't know where to begin."

"The beginning is usually the best place to begin and you may want to start talking soon," she said with a scolding look that did not help Myron at all.

"Baby please, stop. Just listen."

Ah shit, here we go, Hope thought.

"I told you when we started dating that I'd been single because my girl did me wrong…"

This motherfucker better not be about to tell me no bullshit.

"…I told you about her aborting our baby and what not but what I didn't tell you was that she was Chastity."

"What? Chastity? My baby? Wait a minute. What?" she said looking confused as questions bounced around her head.

"I'm sorry that I kept it from you but I was afraid to lose you."

"But-"

"I know you have a lot of questions but there's more I have to tell you," he said with a sigh.

There's more? This motherfucker, she thought as Myron continued.

"I was so happy that you got promoted to the regional head, but I hated that you had to do all of that traveling."

What does this shit have to do with the price of tea in China after you tell me you've fucked my daughter? I swear he has two seconds before I bust him in his shit.

"One night while you were out of town, Chastity and I slept together."

"WHAT?!?!?!?" Hope exclaimed.

Myron continued not skipping a beat, "We've been sneaking around behind your back for the past year."

"WHAT," she let out again.

"I'm sorry that I did this to you, but there's more. I'm leaving you Hope. Chastity is pregnant. We love each other and have decided to be together. I did not plan for this to happen and I am truly sorry."

By that point Hope had completely shut down from disbelief. Myron turned and walked out of the house and left her sitting on the couch alone.

Myron went back to Chastity's apartment after he left their home. Chastity met him at the door. "How did it go? What did she say? Did she jump on you? Oh my god," she frantically asked. She did not go with him because she was afraid.

"She actually took it well. Better than I

thought actually. She didn't say anything."

"That's not good."

"It'll be fine. I promise. Now bring your fine self over here and give me some love." The worry of the situation quickly subsided once their lips locked. "Stop worrying. I got this. Please, don't stress yourself and our baby," he said as he rubbed her belly.

****

Hope sat on the couch for hours after Myron left. She'd cried so much that her eyes were puffy and her face stained with the trails of the tears. She questioned and blamed herself over and over again. The hurt of the betrayal from the two people that she trusted the most was overwhelming.

The sun set and Hope's emotions made a major shift. Her sadness descended with the sun and anger ascended with the moon. She wanted answers and she knew where and how to demand them. She got her purse, her keys, including Chastity's spare key for emergencies, and her handgun.

Hope played out every scenario in her mind that she could think on her drive to Chastity's. "All I know is that they better not come at me with any more bullshit because I need answers," she said once she got to the apartment complex.

Hope was mad all over again when she saw Myron's Jaguar parked in front of the townhouse. "Bitch ass motherfucker," she whispered as she dug her key into the car from bumper to bumper in a steady motion.

She walked to the door and inserted her key. The house was dark, so she assumed Chastity and Myron were upstairs in "their" bedroom. She stopped in the living room, listening for any noises or movement in the house. She heard muffled sounds. She made her way up the stairs to the bedroom. The door was closed; she slowly turned the knob. Once she opened the door, she saw Chastity mounted on top of Myron.

Hope stood there for what felt like an eternity watching her daughter make love to her husband. The room turned crimson. She pulled the gun from her purse and walked across the room to the bed. Chastity said "Oh my god," as Hope placed the gun to Myron's temple and pulled the trigger.

Chastity screamed hysterically as blood drenched the white sheets. She was fear ridden as she looked up at her mother's cold soul-less eye. At that moment, she wished that she never got back in bed with Myron. All she could do was pray that her mother had mercy on her. Hope looked at her as she walked out of the room leaving Chastity to deal with the horror that she had witnessed.

Hope drove home with no remorse for what she had done. Once home she turned her surround sound on and grooved to Jill Scott as she showered to remove Myron's blood from her body. Afterwards, she warmed up the dinner that she had prepared for herself and Myron. Hope had just finished her dinner and a glass of wine, when the police arrived to her house. She did not put up a fight and nonchalantly walked out with a smile on her face.

****

"Ms. Hope your time is up," her nurse Shantel said.

Hope looked up at her and smiled as she said, "Okay."

Her daily garden visits were what kept Hope strong while in the McLaughlin's Women Mental Institute. Hope's lawyer got her an insanity plea that landed her there versus in the state penitentiary. She wished that she was not locked up, but she never wished to do anything differently. She never regretted killing Myron, because she felt that he deserved to die and she had to be the one to make it happen. However, she did regret not being able to have a relationship with her daughter and her grandson. *Oh well,* she thought as she let out a sigh. Hope followed Shantel back to her room where she picked up her notebook and continued to write the story of her life.

Sugar Honey Ice Tea

The cold walls consume me as I lay in my bed; well my bunk, with a two inch thick mat. It was a stark contrast from the luxury of the bed in the home that I once had or the many hotel rooms I'd frequented over the years. Now the only place I visit is the yard of the North Carolina Correctional Institute for Women.

Prison was never where I saw myself. Not the "baddest bitch" Cheyenne Gibson; Miss loved by many and hated by most. I was that bitch that made the party jump. That bitch that stayed fresh from head to toe. I quickly realized that none of that shit mattered once I got sentenced. Prison tends to knock you off of your pedestal.

I can't blame anyone but myself for my misfortune. I've done a lot of fucked up reckless shit in my life. Some shit that my closest friends don't know or probably wouldn't believe that I did. Now that I'm counting down the days until I die, I figure it's time to come clean with my shit. Maybe it'll help the next chick who thinks she's invincible.

They gave me a typewriter to tell my story. The counselor said it's some therapeutic shit to help with my issues. Yeah okay. Well here I go...

****

I was born on January 17, 1994 to Daniel and Sharon Gibson at Cape Fear Valley Hospital in Fayetteville, North Carolina. That was probably the happiest day of my parents' lives. I was their rainbow baby, born after two miscarriages; guess third time's a charm.

My parents were average middle class citizens. Mom was a receptionist at the Holiday Inn and Pops was a car salesman. They weren't millionaires, but my parents provided for me and later my little brother Brandon.

I watched my parents bust their asses day in and day out to ensure that we had what we needed. I was forced to grow up fast because they worked so much. I took care of myself and Brandon because by the time my mom came home she was beat.

I was twelve when I was able to cook a full meal, clean, and keep up with seven year old Brandon. It was a good thing that I did learn some home maker skills though, because tragedy later struck our home.

My freshman year of high school, my mom had a stroke. Her abilities were limited and I had to step up. It was okay though because I didn't have a life anyway. Pops didn't play that going to this place or that place stuff; it was just school and home. That was all. The only exception was going to my best friend Ciara's house.

The only reason my Pops went for that was because she lived around the corner and he was well acquainted with her mom.

Her mom and dad were divorced, so it was only Ciara and her mom that lived at the house. Ciara's mom was a nurse and worked long crazy hours, so when I went there we did our dirt. It didn't consist of anything more than talking freely on the phone with boys for me, but Ciara's hot ass was fucking. All of that changed during my junior year though.

Ciara was dating this dope boy named Prodigy. They'd been kicking it for a while. At first she was just dealing with him for the money, but then she got caught up and dropped the other dudes that she was talking to.

One day, we skipped school and chilled by Prodigy's house. He introduced me to his homeboy Yusef. I melted when he said, "Hey ma." He was fine as hell; brown skinned, green eyes, and had muscles for days.

"Hey," I responded hoping not to show my nervousness.

We chilled and watched TV for most of the day. We'd ate lunch, which was pizza and hot wings, and then Ciara and Prodigy went into the room to get it on.

"What's good Ma?" Yusef asked me.

I knew what he meant but I acted like I didn't. "Ain't nothing," I said with my eyes glued to the TV.

"You want to go in the room? We can watch TV in there," he said hypnotizing me with his words.

I knew that he was going to try me and I knew I probably wouldn't have been able to resist him.

"Come on. I won't bite you," he said. I didn't respond so he added, "Unless you want me to," with a smirk.

"Huh?" I asked sounding petrified.

"I'm just playing Ma. Come on," he said offering me his hand.

I reached for it and let him lead me to Prodigy's second bedroom. He turned the TV on and walked me over to the bed. He moved closer to me and kissed me. He was gentle and his tongue tasted sweet. He took me out of my head and I was ready to do whatever he wanted me to.

"I can't lie I'm digging the shit out of you. I want you Ma. Let me make you feel good."

"I-I-I," I stuttered.

"What? You're not feeling me?"

"It's not that..."

"What is it then Ma?"

"I'm a virgin," I said dropping my eyes to the ground in shame. Ciara hounded me about being a virgin, but the truth was I was too damn afraid to do it.

Yusef raised my chin for me to look at him. "It's okay Ma." I shifted my eyes again. "Listen Cheyenne, I'm trying to really get to know you. I'm not just trying to hit it and then dip out on you. Trust me."

It was like he was hypnotizing me for real. "Okay," I said.

He smiled, kissed me again, and then took my shirt off. I shied away, but he coaxed me along. Before I knew it, I was naked and laid out on the bed. I didn't know what to expect because I hadn't even watched porn prior to that. All of my sexual knowledge came from Ciara and that only consisted of her telling me that it felt good and how I needed to try it. Yusef kissed my lips and slowly made his way down my body. A tingling sensation that I'd never felt went throughout my body. I almost lost my shit when he placed his mouth on my vajayjay. I let out a sound that messed me up. I can't help but laugh thinking back on it now though. To say that it felt good was an understatement. The first time I had an orgasm, I felt like I was having an asthma attack. An hour later, I had a swollen coochie and was in love with him.

Yusef and I continued to kick it after our first encounter. During that time we had lots of sex, and also got money together. Yusef taught me the game. I sent some school kids his way and I ran for him occasionally. We were on our Bonnie and Clyde shit; he had my back and I had his.

Things at home got crazy. Honestly, it was because I started to smell myself. Between getting dicked down on the regular and having a man that was "getting money" you couldn't tell me anything. My Pops wasn't having it though; he put my ass out with the quickness. I stayed with Ciara for a minute until Yusef set me up in a one bedroom apartment. He hung out and stayed over sometimes but he didn't move in, in fear of bringing heat to me or my spot. He spent most of his time at the trap house; which I later found out that it was where Ciara and I were taken when we first met.

Things were straight. Like any relationship, we had our shit about us. I had to get at him a few times about messing with other females, but he always handled business at home first.

We were good for almost a year and a half, before things went haywire. It was a month before graduation and I was getting things together; which included mending the relationship between me and my parents.

My brother and I were at my apartment when I got word that Yusef had been picked up by the feds. I took Brandon home and linked up with Ciara to find out what was going on.

Once we got to the hood, I found out

that he and Prodigy had gotten picked up on drug conspiracy charges. The pickup seemed bogus to me and I'd bet my life that someone snitched on him.

It was almost a week before I finally spoke to Yusef. I was sick until I did.

"I need you to stay focused Ma," he said. "Get your diploma and get the hell out of the Ville."

"But-"

"But nothing. These fools are trying to get me for twenty years. I don't want you to put your life on hold for me."

"I will though."

"I know. That's why I'm telling you this. Live your life and when/if I get out then we can rock again. I'm going to drop a letter in the mail for you, so look out for it."

"Okay," I said sadly. We hung up and I cried my eyes out.

I got his letter a few days later. He told

me not to forget everything he'd taught me and he coded a message telling me where his stash of drugs and money were. I hustled the drugs to the kids at school and to the fiends at the places that I'd made drops at. I was able to live for about six months with the money and what was left in the stash.

I did not leave Fayetteville like Yusef told me to. I was determined to hold him down. He was sentenced to fed time and shipped to Texas. He wasn't perfect, but he was perfect for me; unlike some of the other situations that I got myself into.

****

Yusef had gotten me accustomed to getting fast money. I was not cut out for a nine to five so I got a gig at the local strip club. Shaking my ass was never in my plans for my future, but the money was good. That along with the financial aid refunds that I got once I enrolled in community college took care of me, and more importantly kept me from going back to my parent's house.

The club was where I met Antonio. He came through regularly and dropped lots of money on me. He dropped so much money that I even fucked. Other chicks were fucking in the VIP rooms on the regular, but until then I didn't. Antonio was fine as hell though; not to mention he laid a stack in my lap for the pussy. Shit, think I wasn't going to give it to him? Plus, it had been a minute since I had any. That shit was good too, so don't judge me.

He fucked me up after we were done because he said, "I knew you had that good-good. I need to put you on my team."

"Your team?"

"Yes my team of ladies."

"What are you a pimp or something?"

"No, I'm a business man."

He pulled out a business card and

handed it to me. "Call me tomorrow," he said as he got up.

"So just like that?"

"Exactly like that. I'll be waiting on your call," he said arrogantly.

He kissed me on the forehead and walked out. It really fucked me up how he left the situation. He had me curious and of course I called him. He gave me an address in the Gates Four area. I was shocked because that was where the upper class folks lived.

Antonio welcomed me into his big ass house that was decked out. "Welcome. Have a seat," he said as he walked me to an office.

"Nice house," I said as I sat down.

"Thank you. Would you like something to drink? Water? Juice? Wine?"

"I'd like some water please."

He stepped out and came back with a bottle of water. "Here you go, lovely."

Sugar Honey Ice Tea

"Thank you. So give it to me straight, what the hell are you into with a place like this and talking about a team of women? Sounds like a pimp to me."

"Not a pimp my dear. I'm a businessman. I'm a coordinator," he said with a slight smile.

Get the fuck outta here, I thought in my mind. "Okay," I said slowly. "What exactly do you mean?"

"I coordinate entertainment for events. I have a team of women and men who are hired for entertainment. Everything starting from birthday parties and bachelor/bachelorette parties, to sex orgy parties."

"Oh I get it...so you're a pimp," I said slick before sipping my water.

He laughed at me and said, "No, I'm a businessman."

"So what do you want from me?"

"Like I told you, I want you to join my

95

team. You dance, you're sexy, and you have some bomb ass pussy so I think you'd be an asset to my group. A lot of my clients are looking for dancers for private parties. Fucking with me, what you make at the club will look like chump change."

He sipped on his whiskey and said, "This is an opportunity that you don't want to miss out on."

"Oh yeah?"

"Yes. Listen Cheyenne, either you take it or leave it. No disrespect but there are a lot of 'you' out here, so either you are down or you're not."

For a minute I was ready to flip out on him, but his cockiness intrigued me. That day I got into business with Antonio. I got money like I never dreamed of. I traveled up and down the East Coast bouncing back-and-forth from upscale hotels, lavish homes, and exotic clubs. The money stacked and my invincibility increased in my mind.

I'm not going to lie though; everything was not peaches and cream. I'd seen some foul shit. One time, I witnessed one of the girls overdose on heroin. It was some scary shit. However, it wasn't scary enough for me to stop getting money. I saved up enough money to get me a nice car (Audi A5 Coupe) and a house (five bedrooms and five bathrooms). It made the grinding even sweeter having a nice home to go back to in between traveling. I was rolling. My bank account was stacked and I had no worries. Life was good and I couldn't see anything different for me, until Mario came into my life.

I met Mario at the bank where he worked. I was there to open an investment account. I went out with this broker, who got me to thinking that investing wouldn't be a bad move. However, I wouldn't do it with him though because he was a coke head. Nonetheless, I ended up at Service National Bank. I'd gotten set up and was walking from the customer service department when I was approached by Mario. He was sexy as hell; black and Puerto Rican, caramel skin, hazel eyes, well-dressed, and smelling good.

"Excuse me miss," he said politely.

"Yes?"

"Can I speak to you for minute?"

"Sure. Is there something wrong with my paperwork?"

"Oh no. Honestly, I've been watching you since you walked in and I think that you're absolutely beautiful."

I usually didn't get all excited about compliments but his mouth formed the words perfectly.

"Thank you."

"You're very welcome. I'm Mario by the way. And you are?"

"Cheyenne."

"A beautiful name for a beautiful woman."

"Thanks again."

"I know you're probably busy so I don't want to hold you up, but if you're not spoken for I'd love to take you out for dinner."

I wasn't "seeing" anyone for real and he was fine so it seemed like a no-brainer to me.

"Sure, why not?" I replied nonchalantly.

"Okay then Ms. Cheyenne," he said with a smile.

I think he was probably shocked that I wasn't falling all over him like most women probably did. Any who, I gave him my number and we went out the next night. I really liked him and kept him around for a while. I balanced my time between Mario, Antonio, and Yusef. Mario was perfect and that was the problem. The way my life was set up, I didn't like to take the easy/right road. It was like I was addicted to chaos. Mario didn't agree with what I was doing for money, but I refused to let the money go; that was until Yusef made me. I had received a call from Yusef letting me know that he was getting out early.

"Why didn't you tell me that you had an appeal going on?" I said immediately after the words left his lips.

"I didn't want you to get your hopes up. You're one of the realist chicks I know Chey. I love and appreciate your loyalty baby. With that being said, I hate to keep putting you through the drama that I've put you through throughout these years. You play that tough shit with everyone else, but I know you're sensitive."

"Whatever," I said slick mouthed.

"So when will you get out?"

"Tomorrow."

"Tomorrow? Okay. What time do I need to be there?"

"No time. I'm going to take a bus."

"A bus?"

"Yes. You do remember that I'm in Texas?"

"I don't give a fuck about that. The highway runs to Texas."

"I know baby, but-."

"But nothing Yusef," I said cutting him off.

"I'm about to pack a bag and get on the road."

"Baby…"

"Listen, there's nothing you can say to change my mind. I have the address so I can add it to my GPS. I want to be there to celebrate your freedom with you. So what time are you being released?"

"They said between twelve and two PM. Chey, I really don't want you to get on the road to pick me up. It will be the same effect if you get me from the bus station."

"Whatever. I'll see you; tomorrow."

Yusef huffed and said, "Okay baby. I can't wait to hold you in my arms."

"Me either," I said with a huge smile on my face.

"I gotta go baby. I'll see you tomorrow. Make sure you drive safe."

"I will."

As soon as we hung up, I jumped up and packed an overnight bag. Once I was done, I grabbed my phone to put the prison's address in the GPS. It started to ring. I almost shit bricks when Mario's name came across the screen.

"Fuck," I said because even though I loved him, my love for him was nothing compared to the love that I had for Yusef.

"Hello."

"Hey baby," he said.

"Hi."

"What are you up too?"

"Actually I'm about to leave my house."

"Oh okay. Where are you headed?"

"Uh..." I said debating on if I should tell him the truth or not. "I'm about to go to Texas."

"Texas?" Mario said sounding confused.

"Yes. Yusef is getting out early and I'm going to pick him up."

"Oh, that dude. So you're running back to him?"

I told Mario from the beginning about Yusef and the bond that we shared. He still decided to move forward with me because he thought that we would have been married with children by the time Yusef got out. He was right, because he was the one to make me ask myself, Yusef who?

"Not exactly," I said.

"It is exactly that. You're dropping everything to drive from North Carolina to

Texas to pick him up. Then what? You're not going to drop him off anywhere. Y'all are going to be in there playing house. What about me? Have you thought about that?"

"I did," I lied because I hadn't thought about anyone or anything after my conversation with Yusef.

"You did? Well I guess you didn't think enough about me to rethink your decision. I love you Cheyenne, and for that reason I'm going to let you go. I hope he does not hurt you, but I'm always here if he does. Safe travels," he said before he hung up.

I felt like shit, but I didn't have time to get into my feelings. According to the GPS, I had a fifteen hour drive ahead of me.

I drove all night, and was tired as hell by the time I got there. It was just before eleven AM, when I finally arrived. I entered the building and gave my name and information to the correctional officer. She noted in her computer system which inmate I was waiting for and that I would be in the parking lot. She said that she would see what she can do about getting his paperwork done earlier. I thanked her and went out to my car and crashed for a few because I felt like shit from all the energy drinks I drank to stay awake.

I was knocked out when I was woken up by a tap on my window. I opened my eyes to see, Yusef's fine ass standing there. I hopped out of my car so damn fast into his arms. He kissed me and it was like the first time all over again; it was truly magical. Hell, I don't even remember our conversation or anything. We got a room at a Holiday Inn off of the interstate because I was tired. However, before I crashed, we both showered and got it in. I rocked his world too. He quickly realized that twenty-seven year old Cheyenne was better equipped to handle business then

Situationz

the seventeen-year old Cheyenne he was used to.

Like many times throughout my life, I was reckless that night and the result of it was a positive pregnancy test a month later. Even though I was shocked, it was cool though. We were in love and everything was all good; until it wasn't.

****

Our son Princeton was four years old and Yusef's habits had not died; they were just suppressed. I was working for a real estate agency at the time because like I said, Yusef cut that fast money shit out immediately. While out with a client, I received a call from a young lady stating that she wanted to look at one of my listings. I got her information and we set an appointment to meet at the house later that day.

"Miss Watson?" I asked when the lady got out of her vehicle. She was a pretty woman who appeared to be about six or seven months pregnant.

"Yes, but please call me Alicia," she replied.

"Nice to meet you Alicia," I said as I extended my hand to her.

"Likewise," she said with a smirk.

"Well, let's get started with the walk-through. This is a beautiful house. I must say you have good taste."

"Yes, I like to think so."

We went through the house and she was sold.

"I love it and I would like to put an offer in."

"Great," I said thinking of the commission on the three hundred and fifty thousand dollar house.

Apparently, she was the daughter of a prestigious surgeon and money was not an issue.

"Let's meet at the office to get your

paperwork started. I will call the seller on the way there."

"Sounds good," she said.

We left the house and met at the office. I put in an offer of three forty-five with closing paid by the seller and it was immediately accepted. I was ecstatic!

I congratulated her and we'd finished up when she said, "Thank you so much for helping me get the house. I've been watching it online for almost two months now."

"No problem, that is what I do. I love selling houses."

"I can tell. You are a nice woman."

"Well thank you," I said with a huge smile.

"I have to come clean about something."

"Okay," I said slowly.

"I did not find you by accident. I actually sought you out."

I then had a strange look on my face.

"I know Yusef, and I found you through him."

"Oh okay," I said feeling relieved because I didn't know where her "something" was going.

"Well, we've been seeing each other for a while now and this is our baby that I'm carrying."

"Oh wow," I said stunned.

I was bombarded by emotions at that moment, but the boss in me wouldn't allow myself to be up in there like a little bitch so I replied, "Well, I wish you both the best. I will contact you tomorrow about conducting your closing."

She said, "Okay."

She seemed confused so I helped her out, "Look Alicia, I see the confused look on your face so check it, I'm about my business. This right here is business. I'm going to dismiss Yusef's lying cheating ass to you no doubt, but this 'business' is for me and my son. So like I said, I will contact you tomorrow in reference to your closing. You have a wonderful afternoon."

She walked out and I said to myself, *the fuck she thought was going to happen? I was not going to take her money because she is fucking my man? Ha! Bitch you tried it.*

I cleaned off my desk and then rushed home so that I could get in Yusef's shit. I thought about the whole situation while I drove home and rethought the entire flipping out scene. Instead I made a quick phone call, then went home and fucked his brains out.

When he reached out to me to cuddle I spat, "Don't touch me you cheating bastard."

"What?" he asked.

"You heard me, I did not stutter. Get your shit and go."

"Baby no. I love you."

"I love you too but not as much as I love myself and *OUR* son. I'm not doing this with you, Yusef. I am not seventeen anymore and I'm not going to put up with it. I need more than just good dick from you. So on that note, I'll get at you if/when I want some good dick. Until then, go and be with Alicia and y'all baby."

"Baby, no. I want to be with you," he pleaded.

"Ha!" I said just before my doorbell rang.

"Right on time," I mumbled as I went to the door. "Your ride is here" I said to Yusef, as I greeted Alicia.

He was shocked.

"You need help?" I asked him.

"Chey, don't do this please."

I ain't going to lie, his plea struck a chord on my heartstrings, but I refused to succumb to that desire.

"I didn't do anything, you did. Best wishes to you and Alicia. I'll call you about Princeton and the dick. Good night," I said and walked off.

After about a minute, I heard the door close and Yusef and Alicia left. I cried a little after he left but I knew that it was for the best.

The following months were very rocky. Alicia had her baby (Brooklyn), Yusef and I agreed on joint custody, and I battled my feelings for Yusef (while getting the "D" of course).

It took a little over two years before everything smoothed out; in that situation anyways. I started kicking it with this guy named Carlos. By the time I met Carlos, I was ready to settle down; mainly because everyone around me was happy. Yusef and Alicia were doing great, and Mario was married with children.

After almost a year of playing house

with Carlos, shit got crazy and I landed myself in the hell hole known as North Carolina Correctional Institution for Women. I started to not feel well and almost shitted bricks thinking I messed around and got pregnant so I went to the doctor. I patiently waited on the results of my blood test since the urine test was negative.

I was at my office when the nurse called me, "Ms. Gibson, this is Jamie from Dr. Brock's office. She needs for you to come in as soon as possible."

"Okay. I can be there in thirty minutes. Is that okay?"

"Yes, that's good. I'll let her know."

There was a knot in my stomach the size of a grapefruit. I wasn't ready for another child, but I prepared myself for it. I figured a baby wouldn't have been that bad since Carlos and I had been talking about marriage. I left work and went to my doctor's office. I nervously sat in the exam room when Dr. Brock entered the room. She greeted me and then took her seat.

"Ms. Gibson as you may know per your concern, we took a blood sample to conduct a pregnancy test. I have some shocking news about the sample."

"Okay," I said bracing myself for the news.

"There is no easy way to say this, but you're HIV positive."

"Excuse me?" I said feeling like I'd gotten hit by a bus. "What did you just say?"

"When we conducted the pregnancy test, which came back negative by the way, we noticed some abnormalities with your T-cell count and in turn conducted a HIV test. I know this is a lot to take in right now, but know that with medication you can live a normal life. I have a prescription here waiting for you already. Also, you will have to notify any sexual partners that you may have had in the past six months to a year about your results."

I immediately thought about Carlos and how I was going to tell him. I felt like someone had cut off my air supply. I sat like a zombie as she went on. I finished my visit and walked out with my prescription in hand. I was so out of it that I really don't remember much about the day except that I picked up my medication and had an attention grabbing conversation with Carlos.

Princeton was at Yusef and Alicia's. I was at home guzzling down some wine when Carlos came over.

"What's wrong?" he asked when he saw my puffy red eyes.

"We need to talk."

"Okay," he said looking nervous.

I took a deep breath and said, "I went to the doctor a few days ago because I thought I was pregnant." He tried to interrupt me but I continued, "Today, I went in for the results of my blood test and I was told that I have HIV."

I paused and took a break to hold back my tears before I continued, "So you need to get checked out."

Carlos didn't say anything so I asked, "Did you hear me?"

"Yes, I heard you. It's just that I don't need to get checked because I already know that I'm positive."

"You already know?"

"Yes, I've known for a little while now. I know that I should have told you but I knew that our love could overcome this."

He went on and on about love this and love that, us this and us that, and together...together...together, but all I heard was that bitch knew he had HIV and didn't tell me. After the hundredth I love you, I snapped. I picked up the wine bottle that was on the coffee table next to me and hit him with it. I hit him repeatedly until he was a lifeless bloody mess on my living room floor. Once I came down from my adrenaline rush, I got a slight weft of remorse. Not for what I did to him, but for my son. I knew that I would go to jail and would have to leave him. I picked up my phone and called Yusef.

"Hey Chey. What's up?" he answered.

"Hey. Listen, I did some shit and I need you to hold me down like I did you when you were locked up. Make sure you take care of our son. I-"

"Whoa Whoa Whoa...What are you talking about Chey?" he interrupted. "What did you do?"

Tears fell down my eyes.

"I killed Carlos."

"What!?!" he yelled. "Why? What happened?"

"He gave me HIV and he knew he had

that shit. When he told me he knew, I snapped, and beat him with a bottle."

"Holy shit!"

"I need to know that you got my back."

"Always babes."

"Good. Make sure you bring my baby to see me too."

"Of course," he said still in disbelief.

"Let me talk to Princeton."

"Okay. I love you Chey."

"I love you too Yusef."

I spoke to my baby and told him that I was going away and that he would be staying with Yusef and Alicia. It hurt me to have that conversation with him but I knew I had to because I did not want him to think that I abandoned him. I told him that I loved him and hung up. Next, I called the police and told them what I did.

Alicia hooked me up with a great attorney, named Mia St. John who worked her magic and I got me a five year manslaughter deal. I hated being locked up, but the fact that I'd have a life to live once I got out was motivation to push forward.

"Let's go Gibson, you have visitation!" Officer Hunter yelled.

I take my medication daily and look forward to my weekly visits from Yusef, Alicia, Princeton, and Brooklyn. I had one year down, and four more to go. I gave myself an once-over in the small mirror before I exited my cell to the visitation room. The biggest Kool-aid smile came to my face when I saw Yusef, Alicia, and the kids. "Mommy," Princeton yelled as he saw me. They all stood and embraced me in a group hug. No our family wasn't traditional, but it was perfect to me and that was all that mattered.

Boss Chicks

I knew it was only a matter of time before big bad Harper Peterson would be taken down. I never imagined it would be like this though. My girls and I always had our shit together and were never caught slipping; so I thought. Staring at the barrel of a gun definitely made me rethink that. "Why," was the only word I could muster up to say. However, the "why" fucked me up as I heard it. Daniel...a name that I buried among many others had come back to haunt me.

I've always had a "boss chick" attitude. I handled any and every situation that arose within my crew. My crew consisted of Arianna Francis, Mia St. John, Kyra Adams, and myself Harper.

We were the crème de la crème of women. We were picture perfect physically and held prestigious positions career wise.

I am a stock broker and let me tell you I'm not your average stock broker; I'm known as the pit bull. I kick ass, make money, and never worry about taking names. Arianna is a lead detective with the Charlotte-Mecklenburg Police Department, Mia is a criminal attorney, and Kyra is a banker. We had power in all areas that counted; which worked in our favor seeing as though we were criminals.

I sat in shock as I stared at the gun that was pointed at me. I was not perfect and did a lot of dirt, but I was not ready to die. Especially not like this; by the hands of someone I trusted. Damn karma truly is a bitch. I was filled with regret as I awaited the inevitable.

****

My crew and I are from Richmond, Virginia. The Bryson Court Projects is where the bulk of our crew united. Kyra and I were born and raised in Bryson while

Arianna moved there in the eighth grade. Richmond streets were rough, but we had each other's backs and made it through with minor scratches and bruises. We didn't do any street fighting or gang banging type shit, but we stayed on our hustle though.

We were about the money. During high school we attached ourselves with the dope boys; which was easy seeing as we were fine as hell. By our senior year of high school we'd saved up almost ten thousand dollars together. Though we were project girls we were smart and determined to break the cycle of poverty that we were cursed with and born into. The summer after graduation we moved out of the projects into a three bedroom apartment downtown. It was moons away from what we were used to in the projects. We were all happy.

Downtown living was expensive but we

wanted to be in the midst of the action. We maintained our apartment with the dope money we got from our men, as well as bullshit ass waitress and hostess jobs at local bars and restaurants. Our apartment was our castle. We never entertained anyone there; it was our safe haven. We rocked with it for almost a year when I met Mia and a light bulb came on about how to elevate our situation.

Mia came to the club where I had worked on a regular basis. She stayed dressed in designer clothes and kept a handsome man on her arm. We talked one night after the club and then had brunch the next day. We vibed and our friendship was formed. Mia was twenty four and in law school. That shit in itself was impressive to me, but she was also on her hustle.

Mia came from a middle class home that didn't allow for her expensive taste, so she found ways to acquire the funds. As our friendship progressed I learned those things included extortion, escorting, and robbery. As cute and timid as Mia appeared to be, you'd never think she was capable of some of the things she did. The girl was bougie as hell, but was on her shit. With Mia's help we were able to take our talents to a higher caliber of men. The local museum, exclusive events, and art galleries became where I planted myself regularly to meet new men.

We pussy footed around until I ran across the victim of our first major hit. Daniel Paige was his name; mister sexy white chocolate is what I called him. I was at the museum when he approached me and asked for my name. I told him and we walked and talked for a while before he asked me if I'd like to go out to dinner with him sometime. I said yes of course and we exchanged numbers. We got together the following night for dinner and some hot sex. After that, he was hooked.

Daniel was a very smart man, just not smart enough to avoid me. He was doing well for himself as a broker. The more I got to know him I found out that he had a prosperous cocaine business as well. That was what turned the simple hit into a long term con. I collected all the information I could and everything was set for our big hit.

Daniel and I had just returned to his house after an evening of dinner and dancing. He held me by my waist and guided me through the front door.

"What a night beautiful. Did you enjoy yourself?" he asked.

"Yes love, it was great. I must say, you have some good moves."

"Thought you knew by now that I had moves," he replied as he kissed me on the back of my neck. That shit drove me crazy.

"Mmmmmm…" I said followed by a giggle. Though it was a con, I'd found myself liking Daniel; which was a huge no-no in my line of work.

"Let me lock up and you go wait for me in the bedroom."

"Okay, because I have some moves to show you," I said seductively.

"Hell yeah! I'm for anything that you want to show me," he said before he sent me off with a smack on the ass.

Once in the bedroom I took off my pumps and fitted red dress and posed on the bed in my matching bra and thong set. Daniel smiled as he walked in. He didn't waste any time to come out of his clothes. My mouth watered as I watched him. Daniel was a beautiful man. His body was immaculate and the dick; oh my gosh that shit was huge! He could have easily been a porn star. I'd always heard that white boys had little dicks. Needless to say that, with ten inches, I was both shocked and excited the first time we'd fucked.

Daniel pulled off my panties as he glided his naked body between my legs. I laid there in anticipation of feeling his mouth, because his head game was mind blowing. Daniel didn't disappoint me and from there we went back and forth showing each other our moves.

We went on for over an hour before we passed out. It was just before three in the morning when I was woke up by, "What the fuck?" and a "Shut the fuck up!" I pretended to be shocked all though I knew it was Kyra behind the ski mask with the gun. I jumped and screamed to keep up appearance.

"What's going on Daniel?" I asked in a panic.

"You shut the fuck up too bitch!" Kyra said as Daniel grabbed my hand to comfort me. "Get out of the bed you fucks!"

Daniel started to object when Kyra pistol whipped him. He passed out and Arianna yelled, "Get your ass out the bed," from the door.

"Gone somewhere with that tough guy shit. He's out so let's do this," I said. I got out of the bed and got dressed; adding gloves to my ensemble. "Is Mia in place?" I asked. Mia's role was to collect the valuables around the house that I'd outlined prior to.

"Yes boss lady," Arianna said with a chuckle. She always busted my chops about my bossy personality, but shit somebody had to do it. Not to mention shit always went smooth with my plans.

"Good. Everything is going as planned so Ari you go ahead to the car and have it ready for us."

Arianna did as she was told as I led Kyra to the hidden safe to collect the drugs and money that were located inside. I removed the painting and put in the code that I lifted from Daniel with some surveillance I'd put up without his knowledge. Once I opened the safe I knew we'd struck gold. There were two kilos of powder and stacks on top of stacks of loot. We briefly rejoiced before we started to load our duffle bags. Daniel came to as we loaded the last of the money.

"Harper? Baby what are you doing? I treated you good and this is how you repay me?"

"Oh look at Romeo. All sentimental and shit," Kyra said as she pointed the gun back at him. It didn't stop him though.

"Why Harper? Money? Drugs? What is it?"

"Shut up your fucking whining!" Kyra spat at him.

"I got your whining you bitch! You better kill me or I'll find you Bitch!"

Shit didn't go as planned. At that point I knew he had to die. As much as I hated it, I had no choice because not only did he wake up and see me involved, but he also saw Kyra's face because she'd taken off her mask while we loaded the money. It was a rookie mistake that I had to fix, so I took the gun from Kyra and pointed it at him.

"I'm sorry Daniel, but I can't let you do that. I enjoyed our time together but this is family."

"But Harper-" he started before I pulled the trigger and silenced him. I watched as the impact from the bullet threw his head back on the mattress.

Mia ran into the room and said, "What the fuck?"

"Harp had to do her boy in," Kyra replied.

I was a little shook because I'd never killed anybody, but I knew we had to get out of there. "Alright let's go just in case someone heard that and called the cops."

We got our stuff and was out. Though that day haunted me, Daniel's name was never spoken again...until now.

****

Things took off for us after the Daniel hit. We were rolling in the dough and doing whatever we wanted to. Being the project girls that we were Arianna, Kyra, and I were balling out of control. It wasn't until Mia brought her intellectual lawyer point of view to us that we truly won in our situation. She suggested that we all went to school and got careers. We put our heads together and came up with lucrative degree plans. Once our plan was devised, we used our upbringing to our advantage and got financial aid so we wouldn't have to use our illegally acquired money. We milked Richmond and the surrounding areas for all we could until we graduated.

Then we decided to take root in Charlotte, North Carolina.

Charlotte was different but we quickly adjusted to the city and in our new found careers. I started at HQ Shultz and quickly moved up in the ranks to one of the top brokers of the firm. I enjoyed being a broker, though initially I picked that career path to pay homage to Daniel. Yeah, I'm a sentimental killer. Anyway, business was good; on and off HQ's clock. I stacked my coins and bought a house in a nice subdivision. We were on fire!

Though our daytime lives carried us in different directions, the girls and I made sure that we did not allow this to interfere with our bonds. Outside of the jobs we held, we did mandatory get-togethers several times a month; dinner at a designated place and brunch every other Sunday. We never lost sight of our focus and kept our circle small; until I attempted to include a girl I met at work. Her name was Sara. We clicked when she joined my team so I invited her to brunch. Needless to say it did not go well and it was clear that she was not welcomed; especially by Kyra.

Tension was so thick when Sara and I walked to the table. "Hey girls. This is my friend Sara. Sara, this is Mia, Arianna, and Kyra," I said as the girls said "hi", all except Kyra that is.

"Nice to meet you," Sara said as she stretched her hand to Kyra.

"Who the fuck is this?" Kyra asked me leaving Sara's hand extended.

"Sara."

"Okay. WHO...THE...FUCK...IS...SHE?" she repeated slowly.

"Chill Ky," Arianna said.

"Fuck no. She brings this white bitch up in here and we just supposed to welcome her with open arms? This that type of shit," she said pointing at Sara, "That will get us fucked up in the game. If it ain't broke let's not fucking fix it."

"Stop tripping Ky," I said trying to calm her. Kyra was the firecracker of the group and once she was turnt up, she was all the way turnt up.

"No bitch, you tripping bringing this bitch to OUR brunch. What the hell Harp? This shit ain't cool. I'm out. Y'all enjoy this Mary-Kate and Ashley ass bitch," she said before she grabbed her purse and left the restaurant.

I could tell Sara was shook by Kyra's outburst. However, me and the girls were not. We've seen Kyra set shit off many times. "I apologize for our friend," Mia said falling into her role as the peace maker of the group.

"It's okay," Sara said softly.

"Don't worry about Kyra. She doesn't like new people or surprises. My fault for not prepping her about you coming. I'll talk to her later after she cools off," I said as I sat down. Sara had a seat and we all had an enjoyable brunch filled with laughs.

Afterwards I called Kyra and smoothed things over. We'd been through so much being that we'd known each other the longest, so I never wanted us to fall out. She voiced her opinion about me including Sara and I voiced mine about her being stubborn and selfish. Her main issue was that she did not want to share her friend. I told her that I would keep the relationships separate and we moved on. Well attempted to because every time she could she let me know either, "I don't like that bitch" or "I don't trust that hoe". However, I dismissed it and continued to do what I wanted to do. I could have other friends right?

****

Hind sight being twenty-twenty, I should had listened to Kyra because she had never steered me wrong. I feel stupid as hell right now while this crazy bitch is ranting and raving about Daniel. I didn't even truly know what her deal was.

"I will fucking shoot you if you keep ignoring me!" Sara spat at me jarring me from my thoughts.

"Huh? What?"

"You make me fucking sick to my stomach, you stupid, fake ass bitch."

Shit was getting out of hand and fast. I knew I needed to attempt to defuse the situation. "Why are you so angry with me? I never did anything to you but try to be your friend."

Sara smacked the shit out of me and said, "So you weren't even listening to me!"

That bitch was pressing her luck hollering at me. All I was waiting for was the opportunity to lash out at her ass, because the stupid emotional bitch didn't even tie me up. But I knew I had to play nice at least for that moment.

"You're right and I apologize. Please tell me again."

Sara let out a loud sigh before she enlightened me on her problem with me. She started on some mumbo jumbo about her family dynamic that I gave no fucks about. However I listened even though I wanted to tell her to shut the fuck up and get a hug from someone who gave a fuck.

"You took away the only person that loved me."

"So Daniel was you man and you're mad that we dated? Is that what this is about?" *Yeah, I would never admit to killing him. No way!*

"You are really trying my patience!" she yelled as she cocked the pistol in her hand. "You're still not listening! My brother, not my man, and you didn't just date him! You fucking shot him!"

I wanted to say "no" but looking at the redness in her face and the fact that her trigger finger was itching I elected to stay quiet.

"Oh, you don't have anything to say about that though huh?"

I sat there silently, watching her closely hoping that she'd come just a little closer for me to lunge at her.

"What you didn't know was that Daniel had cameras in his home. I saw the whole thing. You shot him with no hesitation!"

Fuck!

"You left him for dead you cold hearted bitch! He didn't die though," she said as she wiped a tear that fell on her cheek. "Nope. Danny's a fighter. I make sure he has around the clock care, because thanks to you he is nothing more than a hollow shell."

I sat in utter disbelief listening to Sara.

That shit was unreal to me. I didn't know that Daniel had a sister and I damn sure didn't know he had cameras in his house; only the alarm system. My mind raced as I came up with a plan to rush her and take her gun. I would have to be precise to avoid any major injury. I was prepared for an arm or shoulder shot, because anything else may have been hard to recover from. I saw my window of opportunity and was about to lunge at Sara when I saw a slight movement across the room behind her. I quickly became paranoid, because I didn't know if the crazy bitch had called for backup. Relief swept over me when I saw it was Kyra. We spoke with our eyes and I egged Sara on to talk some more.

"I'm so glad that Daniel is not dead. I've thought a lot of him over the years. I hated how things went down. I'm truly sorry. It is so honorable how you have dedicated yourself to care for him. It takes a special person to bring a loved one into their home and care for them. I commend you," I said as sincerely as I could.

"Well thank you. That was nice of you. Funny how a gun can change one's perspective. But anyways, unfortunately my small apartment could not accommodate Danny's needs," she said in a sad tone.

"Oh my. If you don't mind me asking, seeing as I'll be dead in a minute, where is he?"

She paused like she was debating on telling me or not then said, "He's in a nursing home in Gastonia. He-"

"Shut the fuck up hoe!" Kyra shouted with her pearl handled 45 drown.

Sara was startled and tried to turn her gun on Kyra who said, "Bitch don't try it! Drop that pea shooter and back away from my girl!"

Sara gave me a final "fuck you" look

and pulled the trigger. I felt a burn like never before as the bullet made contact with my skin. The impact as well as the shock of being shot sent me on a downward spiral to the floor. Before I connected with the ground I heard another "bang". I hit the ground and everything went black.

****

A day and two surgeries later I woke up in the hospital. I panicked when I realized something was covering my face. I jumped and attempted to sit up, but my body was not cooperating. Arianna and Mia, who were by the side of my bed, came to my aid to calm me. "It's okay baby girl. Calm down. Arianna is going to get the nurse," Mia said in a soothing tone.

Shortly after a red headed nurse was introducing herself to me, "Hello Ms. Peterson. My name is Mindy and I'm your nurse until seven this evening. How are you feeling?"

"My head hurts and my mouth is dry," I attempted to say behind the respirator mask. However, due to the weakness of my voice I gave up after the second attempt for understanding.

She apologized for not being able to understand me and then began filling me in on what had happened. Sara's bullet went through my tri-cep, and then moved through and out of my shoulder. When I hit the ground apparently I hit my head, giving me a concussion. As if that wasn't bad enough I would not wake up after the anesthesia wore off, hence me waking up with a breathing machine in my face. Mindy continued on about my vitals and what-not, but I wasn't listening. My mind was on Sara and if Kyra laid her down.

Luckily for me Kyra entered at that time and I would know for sure. Kyra spoke to everyone and then stood off to the side until the nurse left. She then moved to my bed. "Hey girl. I'm glad you are awake. I was worried about you man."

I smiled the best way I could behind the mask. Kyra leaned to get real close and said, "You get well and don't worry about anything because I got your back. Sara was whisked away in a body bag and after visiting Mr. Daniel and his bitch ass at the nursing home, he was whisked away in one as well." I gave her a slow nod and a big smile. Kyra always had my back and after the Sara ordeal I vowed to never extend my hand of friendship to anyone outside of our circle again. I knew once I healed I would hear tons of shit from Kyra. I didn't care though and would welcome the words with love. As if she was in my thoughts Kyra turned to me and said, "You relax and hurry up and get better because your ass owe me and I'm cashing in. A bitch needs a handbag, dinner, loot, or some shit."

I chuckled to myself the best I could. Some things called for change but the bond that Arianna, Mia, Kyra, and I all had was perfect and in the words of Kyra, "If it ain't broke let's not fucking fix it."

Broken Mirror

Looking at Sage was as if I was looking into a mirror; our hair, clothes, and demeanor all were the same. The only difference was our eyes. Though mine were contacts that matched the green of her eyes, they were different. I saw hurt, sadness, and betrayal in her eyes. I've always heard that the eyes are the window to the soul. Until now I never believed that. *Had I gone too far?* Was the question I asked myself as I looked down at my friend; my sister. As a quick moment of regret swept over me my friend Allison said, "It's okay. Get on with it. Shit happens." With that I moved forward with my plan to take everything from her.

****

Sage and I had been friends since high school when her family moved from Waco, Texas to Aiken, South Carolina. Before meeting Sage I was labeled “the weird kid” so I was pretty much a loner. Our friendship baffled many people to include myself, because we were from different sides of the track. Sage came from a well to do family. Her family moved to Aiken to take over the Riverwood Horse Stable after having three successful stables throughout Texas. Then there’s me, Lacy MacAfee, the daughter of a plant worker and a waitress.

Though Sage had any and everything that she could possibly dream of and I had the bare minimum, she never looked down on me. We truly had a special relationship. I spent as much time as possible at her house because her farm living was totally different from the two bedroom home I lived in. Her family welcomed me from the beginning and considered me family too.

Sage and I were inseparable. I got through high school with her help and before I realized, it was time for graduation. I was ready for the freedom graduation would bring; at least I thought I was.

My mom became ill shortly after I graduated. She was diagnosed with stage four cervical cancer. That time was a blur in my life. It went from her being diagnosed to her dying four months later. My dad was a certified dickhead, so once my mom died I was alone.

****

After my mother died I moved to Charlotte, North Carolina. When I first got there I met Allison. We became pretty close, but she could never be my Sage. Sage came and spent some time with me to help me adjust to not having my mom, but she had to leave for school. She'd decided she wanted be veterinarian. Sage tried to convince me to go to school, but I never really wanted to go to school so I decided I would get a job instead.

I had received a hundred thousand dollars from my mom's life insurance policy that got me along while I got situated in the new city. It took me about six months but I landed a job at a cellular phone company as a sales associate. It was cool. I made money and met some cool people; especially guys. In my spare time I dated and fucked a lot. Don't judge me, I'd lost my mom. Anyways, I was moving along my life in a way content to me. Life to me was all about me, my happiness, and having fun. I couldn't keep a stable relationship, but I didn't care because I didn't want one really. I enjoyed being able to move when and however I decided to.

After Sage finished school she asked me to move back to Aiken to be her roommate. I guess it was to save me because she started the conversation off with, "Lacy don't you think it's time for you to focus your energy into your future?"

I wanted to tell her to go fuck herself because I was happy. Instead, I transferred my job and moved into a two bedroom condo with Sage on the south side of Aiken.

****

Everything was going well with the move. Sage and I were closer than ever, work was good, and I'd even started speaking to my dad occasionally. I still didn't have a steady boyfriend, which was good for me but seemed to bother Sage. She attempted to set me up a few times. She was in a fairytale relationship and she felt like I should be in one as well. Her boyfriend, Chase, was everything. He was sexy as hell, came from a good family, and was a plastic surgeon. I think that's how they met, but Sage would never admit it because her ass and boobs were fantastic. But anyways, I totally understood why she was all on team love. I must admit that I yearned for what Sage and Chase had but I felt like it wasn't written in the stars for me to have a happily ever after. Sage was always the privileged one and I had accepted that.

One day I was lying across my bed watching *True Blood* when Sage tapped on my door. "Come in," I said.

She peeped her head in and asked, "What are you up to?"

"Nothing. Just chillaxing."

"Oh man *True Blood*," she said as she sat on my bed. "Oh my god Alcide is sooooooo sexy."

"Yes he is!

We watched the episode for a while and then she turned to me and said, "I need your help with something."

"What?" She didn't say anything so I asked, "What?" again.

"I don't exactly know how to ask you

this, but...ummm...it's,"

"Just say it already Sage," I said getting irritated with her beating around the bush.

"Well..." she said with an exhale. "Chase's birthday is coming up and I wanted to do something special for him. Well a little unconventional I should say. He had expressed the desire to have a threesome. And-"

"Wow."

"I wanted to give him that and I need your help."

"My help? How?"

"Take part in it."

Shocked was an understatement for how I felt. Who does that? "What? You mean like do a threesome with you and Chase? That's crazy! Why me?"

"Because I don't trust anyone else. Please Lace. Please. Please."

Reluctantly, I said "Yes".

Sage started talking a mile a minute

about being excited to do this for Chase. I sat quietly as she went on and on, waiting on her to shut up so I could finish my episode of *True Blood.* I "yeah" and "uh huh" until she was finally finished. The only detail that stood out to me was that Chase's birthday was a month away. Sage left, and I watched my show until I fell asleep.

****

The day had finally arrived after I talked myself out of going through with it at least a hundred times. Between Sage and Allison I was in a good place about the decision. What kind of friend would I be if I wasn't there when my friends needed me? I took a deep breath and waited in the bedroom for Sage. Sage had the room laid out with candles and rose petals. I heard the apartment door close and I laid on the bed looking sexy how Allison showed me to. I needed the coaching because I didn't do sexy too often. I was more of a "just fuck me" kind of girl. The door knob turned and it was game time.

Sage led Chase into the room with a blind fold over his eyes. "Stay right there baby," she said.

"Okay," he said in a suave tone.

Sage started to undress as he asked her questions about his surprise. "Shhhh," she said as she quickly slipped out of the dress she wore. I got nervous as I saw how perfect her body looked in the matching bra and thong set. Sage looked at me and shot me a smile as she said to Chase, "I hope you are ready baby," and took off his blindfold. He smiled as he looked at the almost naked Sage. After what seemed like an eternity, he looked in my direction.

"Baby, what's going on?"

The confused expression on his face made my insecurities slowly creep up from within. I shifted slightly worried that I'd lost my sexy.

"What's going on is I'm wishing you a happy birthday."

"I'm not following Sage. What is Lacy doing here and damn near naked?"

"Well...I know you've fantasized about having a threesome, so I wanted to give you that experience."

"What? Really? With Lacy?"

"Yes," she said as she began unbuttoning his shirt.

"I don't know about this," he continued as she took his shirt off and threw it on the floor.

"What is there to know?" she asked as she went for his belt.

"It's just that she's your best friend."

"Exactly. Who else better to do this with? I trust her one hundred percent."

"Are you sure?"

"Uh-huh."

"But-" he started.

Sage took his words away by stroking his hardening rod that she'd freed from his boxers. "Stop over thinking this baby. Let's have an exuberating night of passion with no strings attached," Sage said landing soft kisses to Chase's chest.

"Okay," he managed to say in between heavy breathing.

Sage smiled and motioned for me to join them. Once I got to them Chase gave her one final glance for permission. She gave him a head nod and he grabbed my ass and pulled me to him. He kissed me softly as he grabbed my hand and put it on his rod. Still a little nervous I stroke it timidly. As it grew in my hand the excitement of what was about to happen grew. Chase quickly explored my moistening valley before telling Sage and I to go to the bed.

"Take those off," he told us as he came out of his pants. Our eyes met as he watched me. He never took his eyes off of me and for the first time in a long time, I felt beautiful.

That night's sex-capade was amazing. We danced around the bedroom and pleased each other in a way that one could only imagine. It was pure ecstasy. It was like no other night I'd ever had. Though he indulged on two dwellings, his touches were soft, gentle, and full of passion. There was no doubt in my mind that we made love that night and I needed to experience it again.

****

The weeks that followed our rendezvous were confusing and even a little emotional for me. I saw Chase just as much as I did before hand but the interaction was slim to none. I'd catch him watching me every now and then but nothing would follow.

I took my concerns to Allison, seeing

as I couldn't talk to Sage about her man and I having a connection. Allison told me what I suspected which was that he felt the same things as I did but would not act on them if Sage was around; which was always. Before I left Allison, she suggested that I presented myself in a manner that he would not be able to resist. I took her advice and went to the mall and then to the hair salon.

By the time I fixed myself up I felt and looked like a million bucks. I smiled at my reflection as I looked at myself in the mirror. My once long shapeless dirty blonde hair had been morphed into a golden blonde shoulder length bob with highlights, layers, and a bang. I made my way home eager for Chase to see me. I checked my watch and saw it was a quarter to five. He usually made it to the house after six so that left me enough time to make it home, shower, and don on one of the Sage inspired outfits that I'd picked out.

I showered quickly, not wanting to mess up the awesome job the stylist did on my hair, with the water and steam. I put on some pear scented lotion and body spray before going into the kitchen to get a snack and then plop on the couch until Chase and Sage got there.

However, that plan was foiled. I was leaning into the refrigerator when I heard the door open and close. As I stood up and attempted to back out of the frig I was grabbed from behind.

"Hey beautiful," Chase said as he embraced me from behind. "I missed you so much. How was your day?"

I knew he wanted me. His touch warmed my insides.

He nestled his face into my hair and added, "You smell so good."

"Thank you," I said as I turned to face

him. He jumped back as if I'd startled him.

"Are you okay?"

"Yes. Lacy I'm sorry; I didn't know it was you. I thought you were Sage. My bad."

He looked me up and down. Before he could say anything Sage came through the front door, "Babe, I'm home."

Chase inched away from me as she walked into the kitchen. "Oh Lacy, you changed your hair! OMG you look great! I love it!"

"Thank you," I said never taking my eyes off of Chase, whose eyes showed that he agreed with Sage. Pleased with myself I walked out of the kitchen and went to the living room. I made a mental note to tell Allison about my win as I turned on the TV and laid on the couch exposing my freshly waxed legs in the khaki thigh length shorts that I wore.

Chase and I played cat and mouse for about two weeks after that encounter with nothing more than sly looks my way. That was until we shared another intimate moment; which was again interrupted by Sage. I'd finally grown tired of her and her interference. She was standing in the way of me and love. She had to go!

****

Sage's eyes had filled with tears as she laid bonded to my bed. I'd hit her from behind and gagged her before she'd woke in a panic. I'd let my emotions get the best of me so I didn't have a clear plan at that moment. I paced the floor of my bedroom trying to get my thoughts together.

I faintly heard Allison's voice telling me to calm down and stop pacing. Finally I stopped in front of my mirror. I looked at my reflection hoping that Allison would hurry up and return. I closed my eyes and did the breathing exercise that I'd adapted throughout the years. When I opened my eyes I was happy to see Allison behind me.

The calm she always brought me quickly swept over me.

"I don't know what I'm doing Allison."

"You're doing what you have to do. You're a little uneasy now, but that will pass when you are wrapped in your love's arms." I smiled at the thought as she continued, "Now is not the time to have doubts. You cannot have what you desire until she is out of the picture."

"But how?"

"By an unfortunate accident of course. She is going to fall asleep in the tub and drown," Allison said with air quotes. "You'll have to do the drowning here to avoid any resist from her of course and then move her to the tub."

"How would I do it here?"

"It does not take as much water as you think to drown someone. She is already gagged so all you will need to do it pour water into her nose. Be careful not to grab her face, neck, or shoulders too hard to leave bruising."

I listened attentively as Allison explained the importance of not allowing bruises to appear and moving her quickly so an autopsy could not detect foul play. She also told me to make sure I flipped the mattress afterwards as well so the wet part was not on top. I nodded my head ready to do what needed to be done.

"Good. Just remember you got this," Allison said before disappearing. Leaving me alone to handle Sage.

I went to the kitchen and grabbed a pitcher from the cabinet and filled it with water. When I returned to the room I noticed that Sage was still and no longer squirming. *Had I gotten so lucky and the bitch was dead?* I set the pitcher down on the night stand and put the side of my face to hers. I could hear very faint breathing. I didn't know if it was the effects of the blow I gave her, a panic attack, or possibly the gag blocking her airway, but I did not care either way. With her in the state she was in, I felt that I could carry the task out without drowning her in the bed. Especially since I was a little unclear of Allison's instructions.

I ran to the bathroom and started the water in the tub. I then went back to my bedroom and untied Sage. Without hesitation I dragged her limp body to the bathroom next to the tub. Though out of breath and tired from the workout, I did not skip a beat and started to undress Sage in preparation for the tub. I'd taken off her socks and pants when I thought I heard something. I turned the water off to listen and I heard what I assumed to be Chase. Panic immediately set in because he was not supposed to be home for hours, leaving me the window I needed to pull off the plan.

I hurried out of the bathroom to head Chase off before he could make his way there. We met in the living room.

"Hey Chase. I didn't think that you'd be home so early. Is everything okay?"

"Yeah. It was a little slow at the office so I decided to take a half day. I'm tired."

"Why don't you relax on the couch and take a breather. I had something I wanted to talk to you about if you don't mind." He acted as if he wanted to decline my offer. I moved in a little closer and said, "Please," as cute as I could.

"Okay."

"How about a beer? Or wine?"

"Yeah I'll take a beer."

I went to the fridge and grabbed two beers and made my way back to the living room. I admired Chase's sexiness as he sat on the couch. I handed him his beer. "So I've been thinking about getting my boobs done. What do you think about that?"

"Wow, I think that if that is what you want to do go for it."

"I mean what do you think more so in your expert opinion." I pulled off my shirt and asked, "How big do you think I can go without it looking weird?"

"Lacy, I don't know if this appropriate. Where is Sage?" he said as he blushed.

"She's out. What do you mean appropriate? You are a plastic surgeon so who better to ask. Plus, you've seen me naked already."

"That's not the point though. If Sage was to come in here, you being topless may not blow over too well."

Ugh. She is always causing a problem. "She's not going to walk in first of all and second it's okay because of the relationship that we have. You don't have to fight it any longer." I moved close enough to Chase to where my erect nipples were in his face.

"Lacy-"

"Shhhh...it's okay. We'll be free of her soon," I said as I kissed him.

He pushed me away. "What are you doing Lacy? Hell what are you talking about? Her who?"

"What do you mean what I'm doing? I was giving you a kiss my love."

"Love? Hold on Lacy, I don't know what you are talking about but I am not nor will ever be your love."

"You can drop the act Chase, Sage isn't here so you don't have to keep up the charades."

"Charades? Are you fucking serious? I must me getting punked. Where's the cameras?" he said looking around.

"Stop being silly. There are no cameras. Come here honey."

"Don't fucking touch me Lacy. Are you crazy of something? I told Sage that something was wrong with you. She didn't see it but I did. Your hair, your clothes, your eyes, and your interest all changed to Sage's. Now you're here talking about us and love. It does not matter what you do you will never be her. At the end of the day you are still the same trash that you've always been. All you will ever be is a good fuck. I love Sage."

I got so mad hearing the words that were coming from his mouth. I picked up a lamp that was on the side table and hit him with it. He went down but I was not happy with that. I took the cord and wrapped it around his neck. Using all of my body weight I applied pressure until the color left his face. *How dare he do that to me? All I ever wanted was to show him a love greater than Sage's. Sage...* I did not have time to grovel over Chase; I had to finish what I started with Sage.

As I got up to go back to the bathroom a heard a familiar sound. I looked up and there Sage stood with her .380 pointed at me. "Whoa," I said as I put my hands up in surrender.

"Whoa? Is that all you can say after what you've do to me? Oh my god! What did you do to Chase?"

I took advantage of the moment of weakness she displayed and charged at her. I tackled her and knocked the gun out of her hand. We tussled around on the floor. I managed to mount her and banged her head on the floor. She swung blindly at me with no luck until she somehow drummed up enough strength to buck from under me and throw me into the wall. Before I could recover she repeatedly punched me in the face. One of the hits in particular left me dazed and unable to properly defend myself. I landed on the wall with the taste of blood in my mouth and a quickly swelling eye. I couldn't help but chuckle at the fact that I was getting my ass kicked by the dainty Sage.

"You're fucking crazy Lace!"

"Whatever," I said as I slid down the wall. Out of my good eye I could see that Sage had picked the gun back up. "So what? You're going to shoot? You don't have it in you."

"Yes, I am!"

"No you're not. I know this and you know this."

"Yeah, you know that just about as much as I knew my best friend had my back and would never hurt me. I guess both of us were wrong. Rot in hell Lacy!" she said before she pulled the trigger.

My head hit the wall from the impact of the bullet. I attempted to breathe through the pain as I felt my heart rate slow down. I closed my eyes as Allison showed herself. "It's okay Lacy. Just breathe. The pain will soon be over. You did well. You fought for love and that's all that matters. Chase loved you; he only said those things because he knew Sage was listening."

"You think so."

"Of course. Who would be able to resist you beautiful?"

"You're right," I said with a smile on my face as I was consumed by darkness.

The End

The Predator Within
(PREVIEW)
By: J. Asmara

The hooded man walked into the room of the abandoned building with the final of the three bodies. He placed the limp lifeless body into the wooden table topped student desk. He went into his backpack and pulled out a pair of shackles. He connected the shackles to the bottom of the desk and the woman's ankle. He double checked those along with the shackles of the other two drugged women before he collected his things. He slowly moved to the door.

He exited out of the cold, dingy room with no remorse for the women that he removed from their homes. A sinister smile crossed his face as he thought about them waking up in the room, confused, and terrified. He situated himself in the room next door where he'd set up his surveillance center. He stared at the TV monitor and looked at the three ladies.

He looked at the grey haired Abigail Montgomery. The prominent Evangelist Abigail Montgomery was well known in the community. She was on several committees and donated to many causes; local and abroad. In short, she was loved by many; the hooded man not being one of the many.

His eyes moved from Abigail to the beautiful Georgina Whitmore. Georgina was an educator and did well for herself. The twenty year veteran swiftly moved her way from the classroom to the position of principal at the prestigious Worcester Academy boarding school. She also was the envy of many men's eyes at six feet tall, sun kissed skin, gray eyes, long brown hair, small waist, and round bottom. Georgina had her share of men attempt to steal her heart with no luck. The hooded man knew first hand why they were unsuccessful.

The final most recent victim was Zara Walker. Zara was the owner of a boutique. In addition to being a business owner, she was a wife and mother. Her idea of helping the community was attending her son's PTA meetings, and volunteering at the school.

The hooded man's blood boiled as he watched the women. It wasn't until they began to move, coming off of his sedative injection that he smiled in pleasure. Zara came to first and Georgina second. He watched as they jerked out of the fear of being in the foreign place.

They both spoke hysterically trying to make sense of their position. He didn't pay much attention to that and instead watched Abigail who had not moved. *I hope that old bat isn't dead. She does not get out of this that easy,* he thought as he got up to go back into the room. Zara and Georgina hushed when they heard the door open. He'd pulled his hood low on his forehead so they could not see his face only his muscle body that made them both uneasy.

"What do you want with us? Let us out of here!" Zara exclaimed.

"Please mister just let us go. We didn't do anything," Georgina pleaded.

"Didn't do ANYTHING? You did EVERYTHING!" he exclaimed as he took off his hood.

They both gasped and said "Kristoff."

The women did not know one another but they all had their secrets. Secrets that Kristoff planned on exposing; him being the command denominator.

Coming Soon...

About the Author

J. Asmara is an Amazon national bestselling author of several works of romance, erotica, drama and suspense. The Beaufort, South Carolina native grew up as a small town girl destined for great things. As with most people, her life was not always fair, however she endured and overcame adversity. Her passion for writing evolved in March 2014 with her debut novella When It Raynes and she has no plan of stopping.

Website: www.authorjasmara.com
Facebook: www.facebook.com/AuthorJAsmara
Twitter: www.twitter.com/AuthorJAsmara
Instagram: www.instagram.com/authorjasmara
Email Address: theasmara@yahoo.com

Made in the USA
Las Vegas, NV
12 December 2024

13960543R00098